NATTIE KATE MASON

This book is for all the Goddesses who aren't afraid to be themselves.

THE GODDESS OF BLOOD AND BONE

BOOK ONE OF THE IMMORTAL DEITIES

NATTIE KATE MASON

Cover illustration and design by Bethany Gilbert
Interior illustrations by Soft Muse Art

Copy editor: Chloe Hodge, assisted by Aidan Curtis
Series: The Immortal Deities, Book I

NOT ALL FAIRY TALES END IN A
HAPPILY EVER AFTER,
NOT ALL DREAMS HAVE A HAPPY
ENDING.
FOR SOME, THE NIGHTMARES ARE
ONLY THE BEGINNING.
FOR SOME, BEING A MONSTER IS THE
ONLY OPTION THERE IS.

A History of The Gods

In the beginning there was only the Land of the Gods. A land that dwelled within the clouds, its weather perpetually controlled by the elemental God's powers. A relatively small realm to which the Deities were confined. From there, the universe expanded over multiple planes as the Deities' strength and powers developed, and their numbers grew.

Gods and Goddesses of various strengths and giftings— all-powerful immortals capable of creating and destroying worlds—were entrusted with overseeing different aspects of the cosmos. But when power was the only currency worth dealing in, the Gods and Goddesses needed to find new ways to grow their strength, and gain the upper hand over their fellow Deities.

To attain the title of *Ruler of the Gods* was the ultimate prize. Thus, the mortal world was created, and then the humans. A whole new world in which its inhabitants existed for the sole purpose of strengthening the Gods' powers through their misery, worship and praise. Mortals became pawns in the grand plans of the Gods and Goddesses. Wars were waged and power struggles ensued. The Deities' hunger for strength and supremacy became so intoxicating, the wellbeing of their human creations became an afterthought in the schemes they pursued. For what value does an eternal being have if it is not all-powerful?

Archè and Aria were the first and, thus far, only Rulers of the Gods. Day and Night. Light and Darkness. Life and Death. Where Aria was kindhearted, radiant, and warm, Archè was driven by power, his heart cold and calculating. Aria possessed the gift of light, and Archè the darkness. A formidable union, whose power was incomparable to any other.

Each God and Goddess—as directed by Archè and Aria— oversaw a different mortal realm and role. It was decreed by the Rulers that the immortals who had created each human and land could not abandon their creations to the ether after their deaths, knowing their souls lingered on. The ether, otherwise known as the dark abyss, is a realm free of time and life. The black hole of the cosmos where all the lost and forgotten things go. Thus, The Afterworld, The Pitts of Moor, and the Hall of Shadows where the Gateway to the Afterworld lay were created.

Sanctuary or eternal suffering awaited those that passed from one life to the next. The everlasting fates of mortals and immortals alike lay in their own hands. If only they had fully comprehended the enormity of their eternal judgement, many may not have found themselves condemned to The Pitts.

Over the years, since human's creation, wars were waged by one Deity against another, using the realms as their platform for vengeance and power plays. An endless game for reckless immortals with no shortage of time to their existence. Though, like any hierarchy system, not all Gods—despite their claims—were equal.

Archè and his wife Aria, the Alpha Gods, rule over the Land of the Gods, and all immortal and mortal kind. As a show of respect for their fellow Deities and the humans they created, the Rulers appointed their own children in pivotal roles of dominion over the human world and Afterworld. They appointed their only son, Thorn, as the God of War, and their three daughters as Guardians of the Afterworld.

The Rulers' eldest child, Lilith, the Goddess of Darkness, was commanded to reign over the Hall of Shadows, a parallel pocket realm to the mortal world. The realm was like a throne room without walls. A slate floor perpetually shrouded in dark cloud, led towards a dais on which a throne of sinners' souls encased in bone was positioned. The edges of the room faded away into impenetrable darkness. There, she was charged with guarding the Gate to the Afterworld and determining each fallen soul's eternal fate.

The Gate to the Afterworld was not a physical presence in the Hall of Shadows. The soul ferryman would transport the soul via portal to the Afterworld, where the physical Gate to the

Afterworld awaited on the other side. Only through the Hall of Shadows could a soul enter the Afterworld.

In the Hall of Shadows, Lilith weighed each spirit's value with her gift of discernment before delivering their eternal sentence. The Goddess of Darkness granted safe passage to those worthy of The Afterworld and doomed those she deemed unworthy to The Pitts of Moor.

Chiara, the Goddess of Light, youngest daughter of Archè and Aria, whose immortal soul personified all that was good in the universe, was tasked with ruling over The Afterworld. The Land of Milk and Honey, as the mortals often referred to it, was the eternal resting place of those deemed worthy of everlasting peace and contentment. Chiara ensured no harm came to those entrusted into her care, and that families were reunited for all eternity. An afterlife of peace and love. A haven. A realm that continually evolved to meet the needs and expectations of its inhabitants. A realm that had the potential to appear unique to each soul that dwelled within, though the fundamental tranquil landscape remained mostly the same.

Their thirdborn child, Nushka, the Goddess of Blood and Bone—whose soul was tainted with malice and wickedness—was tasked with ruling over The Pitts of Moor, the eternal resting place of the damned. A fiery realm of smoke and darkness. A realm so inhospitable, only the most depraved and wicked creatures dwelled there. A place of pain and debauchery.

Once her fate was sealed, Nushka was quick to crown herself Queen of Moor and created all manner of wicked supernatural creatures that bowed to her evil whims.

Aria struggled with the idea of Nushka existing in such a dark realm for eternity, but her daughter's longing for power had turned her heart cold and unforgiving. To preserve the righteousness of The Land of the Gods, The Pitts of Moor was deemed the only place where she could live freely without doing further harm. An eternity of overseeing a place so dark and unforgiving, only those souls deemed beyond redemption were sentenced. Only those with blackened hearts were placed under her care.

In a bid to return some semblance of goodness to their daughter, Nushka was tasked with a challenge from the Rulers of the Gods. If the Goddess of Blood and Bone could prove herself capable of virtue and kindness, if she could prove herself worthy of rejoining the Gods by redeeming just one of the wicked souls in her care, then after a time, she could return to the Land of the Gods. Another God or Goddess would be entrusted to rule in her stead.

Not a single soul so far, in all Nushka's reign as Queen of Moor, had been able to prove themselves worthy of a place in the Afterworld. As a result, the Goddess of Blood and Bone's wicked rule remained uninterrupted, and she remained eternally immersed in a realm of suffering and depravity, with only the most sinful of souls for company.

⤙«❄ ☽ PROLOGUE ☾ ❄»⤚

Agnes

Her sister's piercing scream reverberated throughout the dungeon's watch tower. Agnes's dagger had found its mark.

Annie's attempts to create further distance between them were futile. With the Alearian steel dagger embedded deeply in her thigh, blood rapidly seeped from the wound. Agnes released a triumphant laugh as she continued to stalk her prey. She was done playing games. The time had come to reclaim the power that was rightfully hers.

Another scream broke through the silence as Annie ripped the dagger from her leg and applied pressure to the wound. So much blood poured from beneath her palm that it would not be long until she lost consciousness. Agnes had done her job a little too thoroughly.

"Give me your gifting or you will never see the light of day again," Agnes demanded as she wrenched her pathetic, quivering sibling to her knees by a fistful of hair. She pressed her remaining dagger to Annie's throat.

Annie groggily begged for mercy, the blood loss having a profound effect on her level of consciousness already. If Annie didn't restore Agnes with her gifting soon, all of this would be for nothing.

A fierce growl from the cell's entrance sounded and Agnes whirled, her sister still begging for mercy.

"What in the realm?!" Agnes cursed, beholding the Alearian mountain cat before her.

Agnes unleashed her sister, tossing her to the side and flashing her dagger at the giant cat, who bared its teeth menacingly towards her in a promise of death. Without hesitation, she hurled her dagger towards the shifter, who easily dodged the blade.

'Fuck!' Agnes internally cursed, trying desperately to come up with a plan of retreat.

Time seamed to quicken as the mountain cat unleashed herself upon Agnes, her movement so quick she didn't have time to react. The weight of the beast was excruciating as she was knocked off her feet and pinned to the hard dungeon floor. It was over before it had even started. Teeth shredded through her throat, tearing her flesh to ribbons, her lifeblood pouring out in rivers. The pain was unimaginable, and then... it was gone. Agnes's vision faded, and her soul passed from this world into the next.

The Hall of Shadows was like a throne room in a black hole; devoid of any boundaries or limitations. Agnes awaited her judgement on unsteady feet in spirit form. Her throat had been knitted back together and all evidence of her other injuries had been wiped away as she passed into the Afterlife.

Agnes fell to her knees as the Goddess of Darkness stalked towards her, having just returned from ferrying a soul to the Afterworld. There would be no Land of Milk and Honey for her; she could see it in the Goddess's raging emerald eyes. The Goddess who would judge her fate glared at her in utter contempt as she made her approach.

"You wretched little witch," the Goddess exclaimed, striking Agnes across the face where she knelt. Whatever enchantments this place had over her soul, it seemed she was now free of pain.

'Thank the fucking Gods,' Agnes sighed in relief.

"Stand," Lilith ordered, and Agnes did just that. She was smart enough to hold her tongue as she did so.

"I have watched you Agnes," the Goddess declared. "I have watched you for many years and over the last year you have become a particularly annoying thorn in my side."

"I'm sorry! I'm sorry," Agnes exasperatedly exclaimed.

But Lilith wasn't stupid, she knew who Agnes was, deep down to her bones. The Goddess laughed at Agnes's pathetic begging, the game they were playing mildly amusing for her.

"Your begging will not save you. I don't need my gifting to tell me where you deserve to spend eternity," Lilith teased as she wrapped shadow manacles around Agnes's wrists and ankles.

"For all you have done, Agnes Brandistone, for crimes against your family and Alearia, you are sentenced to spend all eternity rotting in The Pitts of Moor," Lilith decreed as she opened a dark portal to her left.

Fear overcame Agnes, over-riding every hateful, vengeful thought and feeling she possessed, as the gravity of the situation weighed upon her. She had known it was coming but being dealt that final blow of her sentence... it was soul-changing. From a swaggering warrior to a pitiful, cowering worm. That was how far she had fallen.

"Please Goddess!" Agnes begged. "I can change! I can be better! Please spare me, I'll do anything!"

Her pleas fell on deaf ears.

"Spare me your pitiful cowering. You're the Goddess of Blood and Bone's problem now!" Lilith cackled ominously. Shadows lashed at the Goddess's feet. Her emerald eyes flared.

With a wave of the Goddess's shadow magic, she shoved Agnes through the dark portal to a realm where only fear, pain and torment awaited her. A realm of nightmares and monsters.

PART ONE

BONES
&
LIES

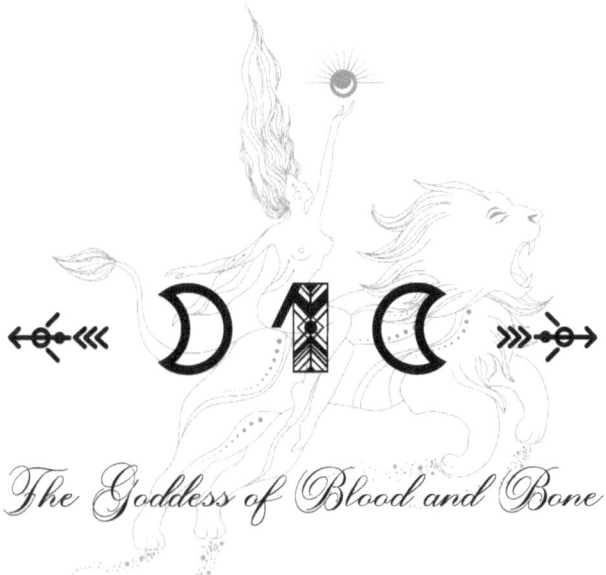

The Goddess of Blood and Bone

When a soul passes from the mortal world into the Afterlife, their senses, along with everything that ties them to the physical world, cease to exist. The ability to touch, feel, smell and taste is erased as they exhale their final breath. All traces of their former lives are wiped clean from their spirits. All wounds, injuries, age lines and blemishes, are expunged from their lingering souls—resembling their former human bodies—as they make the transition from the living to the dead.

The inability to feel pain is a blessing the mortals wish for their dearly departed. A notion that brings them comfort in their time of grief. For the spirits forever coddled in The Afterworld under the care of Chiara, that is the case… as if discomfort is something that should be wholly avoided.

Pain has a purpose; it molds our character. More importantly, fear and pain are potent sources of strength that can be drawn upon, if a Deity such as I, have the inclination to do so. Chiara is weak to restrict herself to drawing upon happiness. Pain and fear are much more effective power sources,' Nushka mused from her throne of bones. 'Even in spirit form, the deceased have the potential to radiate an aura from emotions that can be used to strengthen an immortal. It doesn't hurt that pain is also a powerful motivator, and means of keeping creatures and even long-deceased spirits in line,' the Goddess pondered wickedly.

The Goddess of Blood and Bone lounged on her throne of bone. A gown of soft black silk draped over her slim frame. Her shadows cloaked her shoulders, the sentient power calmly coating her like a second skin, feeling the relaxing effects the fifth glass of wine was having on their master.

Zeri, the Goddess's pet bhoot, lay resting beside the throne upon the dais. The creature hovered, as always, slightly above the ground. On this occasion, Zeri, was in the form of a chimera. The ghost shifter took many forms, but the chimera was their favorite. Zeri's leather wings were tucked in tight. Its tawny beast's body with heads of a lion, snake, and dragon, watched on curiously from their master's side. Bhoots, with their ability to shift form, were usually translucent, as most of the souls in The Pitts of Moor were. However, thanks to the Goddess's enchantment, the bhoot had the ability to turn fully corporal at its master's whim. Though the

Queen of Moor was incapable of love or affection, she found the ghost shifter's company oddly satisfying.

Nushka dislodged an ulna bone from her throne and threw it across the hall for the beast.

"Fetch," she commanded playfully.

Zeri roared in delight with its lion and dragon heads.

Fetch was one of Zeri's favorite games. The bhoot pounced eagerly down the dais steps, snatching up the bone with their lion's teeth. Its dragons head growled in protest at missing out. The Goddess chuckled.

"Patience my pet," she laughed, dislodging another bone from the throne's arm.

She flung the radial bone on a dark wind, which Zeri caught with ease. Not a drop of wine spilt from the glass she held in her other hand. The snake's head seemed unfazed by the whole game, not eager to participate on this occasion. Lion and dragon's heads jutted upright, the beast returned to Nushka's side proudly carrying their prizes. Flopping on the ground, the beast rumbled a purr as it gnawed on the human's bones. Watching the easily contented beast, Nushka smiled softly.

The game over for now, the Goddess was drawn back to her thoughts. The wine of the Gods had a way of making Nushka reflect. As it did for many. It was whilst sipping on her glass of wine, awaiting her handmaidens' arrival, that she mulled over the insignificant details of her life and the realm. Her claws tapped on the glass in irritation. The Goddess's often wild serpentine-like hair, swayed lazily behind her, as if it too were addled by the alcohol.

"Free of pain... Ha! What an utterly abhorrent notion to allow to befall upon your own subjects. A wasted opportunity," Nushka mused to her pet, distastefully drawn back to her previous train of thought.

"What fun would there be, Zeri, in ruling over a hell realm where your subjects could not appreciate the punishments bestowed upon them?" Nushka laughed. "Besides... how else would I renew my strength, if not from drawing upon their pitiful fear and screams?"

Zeri snorted.

Nushka often found herself talking to her pet. Their wicked heart was so akin to her own. Of course, the fact they couldn't talk back was likely a contributing factor as to why the Goddess thought of them with any fondness.

Since her reign in The Pitts of Moor had commenced, Nushka had shown her subjects *mercy*, allowing the spirits entrusted to her care to retain their former senses. This gift was not without its benefits; a fact that her fellow Deities were all too quick to forget.

Originally, the Afterworld had been created for humankind's benefit. However, over the eons, a resting place was also required for immortals whose eternal existence had been cut short. Usually, their demise was attributed to violence.

Each spirit damned to Moor could feel and enjoy all the sinful pleasures they were accustomed to in their former lives, if given the opportunity. The sensation of pleasure was not as potent in spirit form as in corporal form, but they were still able to enact all the experiences they had in their former bodies. Each soul could still have sex, just as they had before. The sensation was just dulled. Though pleasure was pleasure, one may argue. For that opportunity alone, she felt her subjects should worship the very ground she strode upon. But that blessing came at a steep price. With the Goddess of Blood and Bone's *gift* of feeling, they could also appreciate every single ounce of their arguably warranted, eternal punishments.

Some of the Goddess of Blood and Bone's immortal kin viewed her methods as cruel or unorthodox.

"My brethren have no vision, Zeri. They are weak," Nushka trailed on. "They do not possess the ruthlessness that is required to carry out the sentences bestowed upon the fallen."

She went to take another sip of her wine, but the glass was again empty. With a flourish of her magic, another bottle appeared in her hand and she refilled the glass.

"They do not understand me, Zeri, not like you do. They do not understand that the usual laws and moral codes do not apply in The Pitts. Nor do they appreciate what it takes to Rule and survive here. It is a thankless job, being Queen of Moor. None of my kin would last a single day in my position. They would take one look at the volcanic plains; feel the unrelenting heat and be all too eager to return to the luxury of the Land of the Gods. Weaklings. Pathetic, spineless, weaklings."

Zeri ignored her this time, their attention consumed by the aged bones they chewed upon.

"Useless creature," she muttered.

Nushka put the bottle of wine down beside the throne and smacked the bhoot's side. Zeri snarled weakly in response, though the beast wisely redirected its attention back to the Queen.

The wine of the Gods, with its aphrodisiac qualities now humming through her, had the Queen growing irritated with every passing moment she was kept waiting. Thankfully, her handmaidens would arrive shortly, and she would have her needs met. With her free hand she began absentmindedly scraping her sharp claws upon the edge of the throne.

"An eternity of pain and suffering for the majority, Zeri," Nushka spoke. "Time without end, of debauchery and freedom for my chosen few. That is how I rule my realm. The Pitts of Moor; a land of sinful pleasure and eternal punishment, with I as its humble caretaker and Queen."

Zeri's ears perked upright as they roared and hissed in agreement. Bones cast aside, each of their heads now grinning in feral delight.

Through the side entrance to the throne room, in a perfect line, walked Nushka's seven handmaidens, radiating fear and resentment. It was time for the Queen to play.

"Gather round, my pretties. Let me gaze upon your beauty, let me drink in your fear," the Goddess cooed from her throne of bone as she curled a sharp claw towards her handmaidens.

Her emerald gaze appraised each of her servants like dishes at her own personal buffet. Nushka's lips twisted.

'Which one shall I feast of first?' Nushka mused.

With her free hand, Nushka gestured to the room and by extension, the castle around her.

"Did you know," Nushka drawled as her handmaidens slowly approached, fully aware they hung on her every word. "The bones of this castle are a gift from the Ruler of the Gods. A bone from each of the souls sent to my realm, as payment from Archè himself for taking over their care. A small gesture of goodwill designed to placate me. The King of the Gods believes he can confine me to The Pitts for all eternity. What he fails to remember is that you cannot keep a monster caged forever," she spoke ominously.

A shiver seemed to ripple throughout the approaching servants as they fully comprehended just how many bones, and therefore souls, had been sentenced to her care. The numerous bones now thatched together to form the multi-level castle surrounding them, its turrets and towers soaring into the moonless, smoky sky. With each new soul's arrival and bone's delivery, the bone castle slowly expanded, becoming a thing of menacing beauty. A tower in the darkness, illuminated with raging fire pits and a surrounding moat of lava. A bridge of bones connected the volcanic plains to the wicked Goddess's residence. Fissures in the plains revealed bright orange bubbling lava beneath the surface, that could melt skin and muscle from the bodies of immortals, and imbue unrivaled levels of pain to any who encountered it.

From her throne, the Queen of Moor began lazily patting Zeri's soft coat. Each of her appointed handmaidens, clad in their usual uniforms of gauzy liquid night, approached on unsteady semi-translucent feet. They were not blessed with the refinement of a Deity, their movements clunky by comparison, but they would do. Nushka had not appointed them for their grace.

The handmaidens stopped at the foot of the dais, their eyes dropping to the ground as if to avoid drawing their master's notice. The stench of their fear and anxiety flooded the throne room, just as the Queen of Moor liked it.

Nushka deeply inhaled their scents, siphoning their fear and turning it into her strength, feeling the years wipe away from her appearance with each new breath. Its scent barely invigorated her these days—at least not in the way it used to.

"Welcome, my pretties, you all smell sinfully delicious," Nushka teased before taking another sip of her wine.

"I have been waiting for longer than I should have," Nushka cautioned as she scraped her clawed fingers against the glass in her hand. "When I summon you, you are to arrive immediately. If you cannot follow orders, then I will find other handmaidens who can," she warned. Her piercing emerald gaze surveyed each of her servants.

Zeri's lion head huffed a grumbling laugh, the snake and dragon heads seeming inclined to agree, watching their master's prey with predatory keenness.

Nushka's long, black serpentine hair swayed idly around her waist, as relaxed as its master. Her hair was not actually made of snakes as Medusa's was. It held no magical abilities. It could not turn its victims into stone. Yet it was as much a living part of her as her heart; writhing and behaving in such a way that it appeared as if it were a bunch of snakes, reflecting its master's mood.

The Dark Queen's shadow power swirled around the hem of the onyx form-fitting gown that clung to her slender frame. A blanket of her shadow power hovered around the throne's base, begging to be unleashed. The sharp, obsidian painted claws of her free hand absentmindedly scraped along the arm of the bone throne.

"Perhaps you need reminding of who it is your serve, if you are willing to be so tardy," the Queen of Moor mused in wicked delight. "You do not want to risk incurring my wrath…"

The handmaidens whimpered their prayers for forgiveness, to which the Deity rolled her eyes.

"Cease your meaningless begging," Nushka spat.

Silence enveloped the room.

After tedious eons of exitance, with little change of pace or variation, Nushka grew tired of the unending boredom and feelings of numbness. To feel any genuine emotion was rare and prized by the long-lived Deity. Even the sex was not enough. The carnal pleasure only fleetingly made her feel alive: a momentary relief. Too soon, though, did the feelings dissipate, leaving her craving more. Craving life.

As she appraised each of her seven handmaidens in turn, sizing up her prey and appetite, the rogue scent of defiance drifted towards her. The aroma filled her immortal being with hunger and resolve. A challenge one bold handmaiden presented. Her predatory instincts locked upon that scent, all-consuming, deliciously enticing.

Nushka answering grin was untamed.

"Hello, Agnes."

"Your Majesty," the handmaiden replied as she dropped into a half-hearted curtsy. The insolence did not go unnoticed.

It was that point of difference, that fire still raging within her that had drawn the Goddess's attention initially. It was one of the main reasons Nushka had appointed the fallen soul into her service upon her arrival into Moor. How many years ago was that now? Time had lost all meaning, but Nushka was sure it had not been long. Maybe five or so mortal years?

"Agnes the ungifted, the mortals once called you," Nushka recalled with a cruel smile. "The common folk had whispered the name like a taunt. A vengeful mind conqueror disguised as a pitiful excuse of a Princess. A Royal with an appetite for payback and sacrifice, much like myself I suppose. A kindred spirit of sorts, you and I," Nushka mused.

"Yes, Your Majesty," Agnes acknowledged tensely.

The other handmaidens listened with bated breath. Nushka's grin widened, fully aware she had hit a nerve.

"Your arrogance was your undoing. You met the poetic end you deserved," she stated, reveling in the chance to get beneath her skin.

"Yes, Your Majesty," Agnes seethed. Fire raged in her gaze.

It was Agnes's defiance, her anger, that tasted like rich wine upon the Goddess's lips. The way the handmaiden resisted Nushka's thrall and occasionally challenged her whilst they were alone, left the Deity wanting more after each dalliance. There was something about her that the Goddess of Blood and Bone could not get enough of. Agnes was the potential cure for her apathy, or if not a cure, a temporary answer to Nushka's unholy prayers.

Agnes's peaked breasts were framed magnificently by the gauzy delicate uniform of the handmaidens. Her slender form and long blond hair, even in spirit form, inspired heat within the Dark Queen's core. But it was her eyes—the piercing brown gaze, the animosity and fire that smoldered even in death—that was her true allure.

The handmaiden was not particularly beautiful. In fact, by mortal standards, she would be considered quite plain. She was pretty, yes, but not striking by any means. And yet... the passion within her raged unlike any other. Her uniqueness compelled the

Goddess to pursue her like a moth to a flame. If Agnes had fawned over her from fear like the rest, Nushka would have likely grown bored of her by now.

The shadows around Nushka's feet unfurled in anticipation, sensing the Deity's heat rising from within.

"Agnes," Nushka summoned with a hint of amusement, lifting her other hand from her pet before scraping her claws tauntingly against the arm of her bone throne.

The former mortal Royal, reduced to a mere spirit handmaiden, jutted her chin. The sharp, piercing eyes that Nushka had grown so accustomed to met her own emerald gaze, promising something more.

"Yes, Your Majesty," she daringly drawled, likely anticipating another onslaught of insults.

"You and I are going to play," the Goddess of Blood and Bone decreed, her sharp teeth gleaming in wild delight.

The handmaiden sighed. "As you wish..."

As the Goddess of Blood and Bone rose from her throne, the remaining handmaidens dropped into reverent bows. The shadows at Nushka's feet tensed in anticipation, the atmosphere in the throne room suddenly taut.

Agnes

The volcanic plains of The Pitts stretched out from the Goddess's seat of power, the overpowering smoke and ash filling the air causing Agnes to gag. All manner of nightmarish winged beasts, including chimera and the colossal fire-breathing, venomous snake dragons—the peuchen—soared through clouds of billowing smoke, patrolling Nushka's domain. Their expansive, booming wings were like silhouettes amongst the flashes of lightning that cracked through the smoky night sky.

The vibrant glow of the lava and white flashes provided the only natural light in this hell realm. The heat it radiated felt scorching against the handmaiden's spirit.

"How these creatures can tolerate the heat and smoke I cannot fathom," Agnes mused to herself. "Perhaps their thick hides or hard scales protect them."

Whilst in spirit form, Agnes couldn't technically be harmed by the elements—or the lava for that matter—though the heat, pain, and smell still felt as real as it would have if she were still human. Each sensation, as Agnes understood it, was a well-fabricated illusion, *gifted* to her from the Goddess of Blood and Bone upon her arrival into Moor. Her new *gift* was a mockery of the mind conqueror gifting she had received from the Gods in her mortal lifespan.

A peuchen guard slithering around the castle on patrol, caught Agnes off guard and tripped her with a thrust of his barbed tail. She crashed hard to the ground, landing on her behind. The impact of the barbs swiping her skin caused her to hiss in pain, though the action didn't leave a physical mark.

"Fucking son-of-a-serpent!" Agnes cursed, making a vulgar gesture.

"Shuttt yourrr filthhhy mouthhh, whorrre, or I'lll shuttt ittt forrr youuu," the guard hissed telepathically.

The peuchen's mode of communication was also a handy way of getting away with underhanded jabs.

"Obnoxious prick! If I still possessed my mind conqueror abilities, I'd make you pay!" Agnes yelled. "I'd make you all pay," she trailed off under her breath, then got up from the ground with as much dignity as she could muster.

She forced herself to walk away, needing to create some distance between herself and the entitled guard.

"Eternity's looking pretty bloody bleak indeed. I don't know why Nushka keeps me around. I fucking hate my life," Agnes groaned to herself.

'Other than tending to my own needs, I'd had no experience with a woman before Moor. I still don't know what I'm doing most of the time. It's a far cry from fucking Sir Riley amongst the rose gardens back home. I'm not a pushover like the others. Perhaps that turns her on.'

"As a human I was a lion disguised as a mouse, sizing up my prey. As a spirit, I suppose little has changed," Agnes shrugged.

The equivalent of five mortal years had passed since she had entered the Afterlife. Five long years where each day felt like a year and each year felt like a century. Five years of tending to her Goddess's every *need* and sinful pleasure. Five years in which her heart had further hardened and her anger had only grown.

'Long ago my melancholy morphed into the depression that now holds me in its grasp. I used to fight it with all I had, but now I yield to its call. The dark monster zaps all your strength and when you have nothing left to give, it takes some more. The black hole in my mind is so deep that there is no end in sight. I couldn't care less for my own safety or what happens to me.'

"Ether take my soul and be done with it!" Agnes prayed to the stars obscured by the smoky sky and to the universe. But not the Gods. She would never pray to them again.

Only her intrenched survival instincts prevented her from doing anything brash.

Anxiety stirred in Agnes's blackened heart, deepened by not knowing if or when she would grow out of the Goddess's favor. Her greatest fear was that one day she would morph from the source of the Goddess's pleasure, to that of her sadistic amusement. The realm's inhabitants all knew just how quickly the Goddess grew tired of her playthings.

'Two handmaidens since my appointment have mysteriously been replaced. One day they were there and the next they were not. A shiny new soul left in their wake as if they had been there all along,' Agnes recalled. *'Perhaps someday Nushka will move our antics from the bedroom to one of the many torture chambers instead. Both settings are forms of pain and punishment in their own ways. Both require a strong will to endure.'*

"A position of honor," a fellow handmaiden described their role as.

"How lucky we are to have garnered the favor of such a beautiful, immortal Deity,'" another had told her.

Both instances Agnes had caught the slight tremble from fear in their voice. Fear was the only motivator for such lies.

Agnes was angry more than anything. Livid, for being treated as a plaything rather than the prize Royal Princess she was—deprived of the power she deserved.

It was after another long session of satisfying her Dark Queen's needs that had left the handmaiden with renewed hunger for power and revenge. From a mortal life of living in her *gifted* siblings' shadows, to an eternity serving a Goddess who was more beast than woman. She wanted more.

Agnes stopped at the end of a balcony overlooking the volcanic plains. Alone for a moment. A rare opportunity.

"After five long years I'm done," she vowed to the sky. "I can't take it anymore. For too long have I bowed to others and been denied of my rightful place at the seat of power. I am a Queen without a crown and that has to change."

As Agnes looked out over the plains from a platform of bone, an idea began to form. A small thought blossomed, twisting and developing into something more. An idea inspired by the High Witch's rise to power. A plan to settle debts—old and new. A risky move with the potential to damn or save her forever. A spark of hope reignited within her. A feeling so wholly unfamiliar that she almost couldn't place it.

"The greatest rewards require greater risks," Agnes vowed to the cosmos. "Things have to change, and I will go as far as it takes to claim the power that I deserve. I will take control of my own destiny. This will not be my fate."

$$\leftarrow\phi\text{-}\langle\!\langle\!\langle \quad \mathcal{D} \; 3 \; \mathcal{C} \quad \rangle\!\rangle\!\rangle\text{-}\phi\rightarrow$$

Agnes

The bone horns sounded from the castle's soaring turrets; a signal that the nightly festivities were about to commence.

Agnes released a frustrated sigh. "How can it be that time already?!"

Straightening her shoulders, Agnes took a deep breath and prepared herself internally for battle. Depending on the Queen of Moor's mood, the evening's entertainment would result in debauchery, pain, or both. Usually, the Goddess took pleasure in both.

The majority of those sentenced to Moor lived each day in a perpetual cycle of pain and torment. For the Goddess's chosen, eternity offered a little more variation and pleasure. Fortunately for Agnes, she fell into the latter category.

The nightly gathering in the Hall of Bone was an escape of sorts; an unleashing for many of the Deity's more wicked creations.

Immortals, creatures, and departed souls alike, each tread a slim line between pleasure and pain. They treated each moment as if it would be their last, and for the inhabitants of Moor, that very well could be the case.

A peuchen guard slithered out onto the balcony behind Agnes, no doubt looking for stragglers that had yet to heed the horn's summons.

"Gettt a mooove on ssslavvve," the peuchen hissed mind-to-mind.

Agnes rolled her eyes.

"I'm going, I'm going..." she moaned, begrudgingly leaving the relative peace of the balcony.

"Hurrrry," he hissed from behind her. *"You mussst not keep the missstresss waiting."*

Agnes shoved her hand in the air giving him a filthy gesture as she walked away. He was right though. If she didn't get down to the hall soon, there would be consequences.

As a human, Agnes had theorized that spirits could float or soar through the air. Free to roam wherever and however they saw fit. That may be true of those in The Afterworld—she had no way of knowing—but here in The Pitts of Moor, each fallen soul remained bound to the laws of gravity. As she descended the thousand steps one at a time, she relished the arduous journey that afforded her the opportunity to avoid the summons for just a little longer.

With each step that drew Agnes closer to the Hall of Bone, she reminded herself there were worse ways to spend eternity than being one of Nushka's servants. The Goddess could make her eternity truly unbearable if she so desired. She considered herself fortunate, to not yet have incurred Nushka's wrath.

Agnes entered the Hall of Bone through the servants' side entrance and skirted along the wall, keeping to the shadows.

"Get out of my way," she hissed at a couple of souls fondling each other as she tried to make her way to the back of the room.

"Fuck off whore," one of the two males spat at her.

Agnes jutted her chin as she pushed past the pair without sparing them a second glance.

'Never let them see you squirm. That was the first lesson I learnt after arriving in The Pitts,' Agnes recalled. *'It only gives their words power.'*

The fallen Royal found these gatherings arduous. She spent most evenings trying to melt into the shadows to avoid drawing the attention of the Goddess or other foul creatures. After the formalities of the evening were over, she usually sought out some semblance of enjoyment from the buffet of fallen souls. Claiming some small slither of pleasure for herself in an otherwise undesirable existence.

Agnes gazed around the room, on the lookout for a suitable male to ride until her needs were satisfied, or as close as they could be in this form. Just one of the ways she made *the best* of the situation…

Agnes released an exasperated sigh, clenching her fists.

"Bloody brilliant! Can this day get any worse?" she groaned. "I am not in the mood to share."

Coming up short, Agnes dejectedly resumed weaving her way through the room, aiming for the shelter of the shadows that lined the far wall. Her top lip curled as she dodged puddles of spilt wine and all manner of bodily fluids.

On a typical night, The Hall of Bone—sometimes referred to as the great hall—was filled with the Goddess's prized fallen souls. A small cohort of nightmarish creatures and on the odd occasion, representatives of the Goddess's allies would also be in attendance.

The Goddess was drawn to both male and female company. She did not declare her preference for one form over the other. Though she only collected attractive maidens into her permanent service.

On occasion when Nushka craved variety, she would welcome a young, departed army general or highly gifted male into her chambers. It was not unheard of for the Queen of Moor to keep company with visiting guests or allies. In most instances, a handmaiden was also called upon to tend to the Goddess in tandem. The handmaiden tasked with pleasuring both Deity and guest alike. Sometimes the Goddess would summon a pair just so she could watch as they fornicated, drawing her own pleasure whilst she witnessed the carnal engagement. Nothing and no one was off limits in The Pitts. Allies was a murky word, however, for what they were. Neither side meant good will towards the other, but their mutual blackened hearts bound them together against their common enemy—the Rulers of the Gods—who strived to contain them.

Agnes grimaced as she ran a translucent hand over the gauzy black fabric draped across her frame, leaving little to the imagination. The standard uniform of the Goddess's handmaidens, a symbol of sorts to those around of whom she *belonged* to. There was no rule that stated a handmaiden could not engage in carnal relations with others, and Agnes often did. But it was an unspoken rule that they should remain discreet about it or else risk the Goddess's wrath.

Shadows danced over the bone walls from the many burning hearths. Agnes edged her way to the far corner of the hall, concealed mostly from view by a group of ghouls. A shiver trailed down her spine.

Ghouls were unpredictable monsters. Their foul stench radiated off them in waves. Their kind were creatures of nightmares with a fondness for gorging on human souls. The ghouls were humanoid in shape, their frame gaunt, their skin and muscles translucent and rotting. Dark, soulless pits replaced eyes, their mouths a mess of jagged teeth. Agnes was begrudgingly grateful for her uniform, which made her off-limits to the more fearsome creatures before her.

It was only whilst Agnes pondered the protective nature of her whisper of a gown, that she noted how strange it was for such a large cohort of creatures to be in attendance. The only time Agnes could recall such a large group was to mark the Goddess's anniversary as Queen of The Pitts of Moor. Perhaps tonight was to be more treacherous than usual, for what other reason would the Goddess have to have summoned representatives from all her allies?

"Our master will be here soon," one of the ghouls cooed to his kin, his tone cold. Agnes felt her useless heart begin to race. "I can feel him…"

"They are all here. All the key players of old," another added.

Agnes wrung her fingers as she tried desperately to overhear the remainder of the conversation, eager to learn whatever she could, but they walked away. Rather than risk earning their notice and wrath, she stayed where she was.

Upon the dais of the Hall of Bone, the Goddess of Blood and Bone's throne was positioned front and center. Its twin awaited her in the throne room. On either side of the throne, several smaller seats had been arranged. Agnes could not recall ever seeing the dais arranged as such. Pessimism and curiosity stirred within. For the Goddess to share her stage with anyone was inconceivable.

A fellow handmaiden with a similar preference for hiding amongst the shadows approached her. The familiar black gauzy gown accentuated her voluptuous curves. The maiden flicked her curly locks as she often did when she was feeling particularly confident. It was not uncommon for handmaidens to gather in pairs. Safety in numbers.

The handmaiden, Kayla, offered her a small smile as she approached, the gesture so at odds with their surroundings. There was a sense of goodness about the fellow handmaiden that didn't belong in The Pitts. Though she knew it was likely an act that served her purposes. A mask just like the one Agnes wore. All souls were sent to The Pitts for a reason.

After skulking around the group of ghouls, the other handmaiden came up to lean against the wall by her side.

"Did you hear the news?" Kayla whispered in Agnes's ear, acting like an old friend sharing a juicy piece of gossip.

Agnes clenched her fists and bit her tongue, trying to suppress the urge to wring the girl's neck. She was not in the mood for guessing games.

"What?" Agnes asked blandly.

Kayla ignored her lack of enthusiasm. "I heard it from Agatha. She was summoned earlier to entertain Nushka's guests…"

Agnes gulped. "Which guests?" She asked, her interest peaked.

"What is it worth to you?" Kayla asked shamelessly.

"Of course, there's a fucking catch," she muttered.

The other handmaiden quirked her eyebrow, a small smirk drawing across her face. "Come on, Agnes, nothing is free in this place," she drawled.

"Isn't that the truth." Agnes rolled her eyes. Before she could consider the implications of her offer, she blurted: "I'll offer to tend to Nushka tonight… It'll guarantee you a night off."

A sigh of relief escaped Kayla's lips. "Deal," she agreed. "Well… Ilbis is here, Hyacinth too. All the leaders of Nushka's allied beasts and beings. There is talk of a rebellion against the

Gods, Agatha heard it straight from Ilbis himself. Can you believe it?!" she exclaimed.

"Holy fuck," Agnes breathed.

"I know…" Kayla sighed. "Anyway, best be off, take care of yourself. Make sure you hold up your end of the bargain," she warned.

Agnes frowned as she returned to surveying the room. Kayla disappeared, likely off to find another handmaiden to trade the information with while it was still news.

All around Agnes, exotic creatures and immortal beings of myth and legend made themselves at home amongst the castle's usual spirits, *the chosen ones*. The potent smell of urine and wine was so strong that it almost made the handmaiden gag. If she were human, her stomach's contents would have already decorated the already dirty slate floor, adding to the revolting mess of all manner of fluids.

Nearby, a young chimera with talon-tipped wings tucked in tight plowed his mate irreverently in the shadows. The beast, so fixated on his task, was unfazed by the pool of wine that spread at his clawed feet as the surrounding spirits indulged on wine that they could taste but not absorb. The strong blood-red liquid they swigged fell right through them, sloshing in a pool upon the slate floor.

Bored, Agnes watched the evening's excessive revelries continue while she contemplated the news she had heard.

A pleasure palace was what the hall would become after the formalities were over with... had already become for more than a few, she noted. The scent of need and want flooded the stifling air, even rivaling the smell of the floors. A pleasure hall she had hoped to revel in if a suitable male could be found. Her unsated need rising within was making her irritable. Cursing, she rubbed her thighs together to try and take the edge off the tension building within.

"Fucking hell, what I'd give for a man beneath me," she muttered to herself.

A nearby fallen soldier turned at her statement, his eyes raked greedily over her body.

"I would be happy to oblige," he cooed. "But I rather like my balls where they are. And I'm sure Nushka would have them cut off she caught me tangled up with you."

"Get lost prick!" Agnes spat back. "I don't belong to her."

The soul huffed a low laugh. "Keep telling yourself that Princess," he chuckled as he turned from her and disappeared amongst the crowd.

"Arsehole," Agnes yelled after him, repeatedly clenching and relaxing her fists.

The sex was a balm in her spirit form, but it was enough to sustain her. It grounded her, reminding her that even in Moor, not all was lost. Even if the setting was akin to fucking in a dirty ally.

The horns sounded again, sending a resounding echo throughout the hall. The crowded room of spirits and legendary beings fell silent as the atmosphere in the room changed. Those few living immortals in attendance held their breath as Nushka, the Goddess of Blood and Bone, made her entrance upon her pet Zeri. The bhoot had chosen to present themselves in the form of a mighty cerberus this evening.

Each of the bhoot's three ferocious heads snapped and snarled their jagged teeth. Long, razor-sharp claws scraped across the stone floor as the creature with muddy brown fur proudly carried its master, padding its way towards the centre of the dais.

The Goddess was dressed in a gown of midnight-coloured silk that draped over her frame like a curtain of night. She slid down her pet's side with a fluid grace that could only be achieved by a long-lived Deity. Nushka, to Agnes's surprise, patted each of Zeri's heads with such tenderness, careful not to sink her own sharp claws into the beast's coat, before perching herself upon the throne of bone. The affection she displayed towards the bhoot was likely the only warmth the otherwise black-hearted Deity ever showed towards anyone or anything.

The Goddess's dark power, no longer leashed, oozed off her thin frame like a second skin, draping the surrounding floor in a cloud of darkness. Her hair shone like liquid night, swaying gently down to her hips like a living thing. Nushka's icy emerald gaze momentarily found Agnes before returning her attention to the gathered guests... as if they were only now worthy of her acknowledgment. Her painted claws and fangs remained fully extended.

Agnes found the Deity's ability to always know her whereabouts unnerving. Even hidden amongst the packed hall of guests, Nushka had known exactly where to find her. Agnes's breathing quickened. No matter where she was, or what she was doing, the Goddess somehow always knew.

The atmosphere in the hall changed, and despite the volcanic plains surrounding the castle of bone, the temperature seemed to drop as the Goddess and her entourage made their elaborate entrance. Never had Agnes witnessed such a procession.

To Agnes's surprise, Kayla slipped behind the group of ghouls and joined her in the shadows to watch the pageantry.

"How many handmaidens sold their souls for your gossip?" Agnes teased under her breath.

"Ha! Enough to make it worth my time," Kayla boasted in hushed tones, whilst playing with one of her curly brown tresses.

Agnes quirked a small smile.

"How entrepreneurial of you," Agnes scoffed.

Kayla elbowed her playfully in the side. Agnes suppressed a laugh, keeping her eyes upon the dais.

"All hail the Queen of Moor," Eshu, the mediator between the mortal and immortal realms announced during the handmaiden's attention.

The hall's inhabitants bowed in reverence.

"All hail the Queen," Agnes and the crowd echoed in a rare moment of civility. Agnes and Kayla dropped into reverent curtsies.

"Presenting His Majesty, the Peuchen King, Xanos," Eshu proclaimed.

"All hail Xanos," the crowd echoed.

Xanos hissed in acknowledgment. Too big to fit upon the dais, he slithered in through the side entrance and took his place towering over the audience by one of the bone walls. The peuchen, an ancient dragon race, were created by the Dark Goddess and Medusa, the immortal Gorgon herself. The first dragons. The telepathic species with a predilection for human blood, traversed between the mortal and immortal realms. Paralysis awaits those stupid enough to dare look them in the eye. Their kind were also capable of breathing fire, their saliva venomous.

"The stories say," Kayla whispered eagerly, "that Medusa herself, the Peuchen's part creator, was banished from Moor by Nushka. Banished but not killed. Perhaps she could not bear to rid the universe of a creature so magnificently wicked. A kindred spirit. A former lover perhaps?" She chuckled.

Agnes smothered a laugh in response.

"Shhh Kayla! You'll get us into trouble," Agnes reprimanded her.

"Ha! As if we aren't perpetually fucked anyway," Kayla mocked. "Lighten up Agnes, she can't hear us from all the way back here."

"She has ears everywhere," Agnes cautioned, taking an unsubtle step away from her fellow handmaiden. Souls were erased from eternity for spreading far less scandalous gossip…

The Peuchen King tucked in his wings protectively, his onyx scales shining in the firelight. His muscled body was akin to an anaconda. He bore deep crimson colored wings and vibrant green eyes. The majority of Nushka's creations and allies possessed green, glowing eyes. A sign of unholiness. A sign of Nushka's favor. With his wide mouth, sharp fangs, and a long-forked tongue permanently stained red with the blood of its victims, Xanos hissed at anyone who dared glimpse in his direction. None dared to look it in the eyes, fully aware of their fate if they did. For even souls long deceased would meet the same fate as the living.

"Presenting Mandigon, of the edimmu clan," Eshu announced as the procession continued.

"All hail Mandigon," the crowd declared. Their volume and enthusiasm waning.

"All hail Mandigon," Kayla whined.

Agnes glared at her in reproach and Kayla merely rolled her eyes and smiled sweetly.

"You need to relax Agnes, or you'll grow wrinkles," she joked and at that Agnes couldn't help but smile.

"I'll relax when Moor freezes over," Agnes replied dryly.

Mandigon, leader of the edimmu clan, took his place at the Goddess's left. The leader of his species resembled an emaciated human form, with cerulean tinged skin and flaming red eyes. The edimmu species resided in Moor, but gained their strength from breathing in the spirit and life force of humans in the mortal realm. Their method of feeding was akin to the ghouls.

"He's looking a little blue. Don't you think?" Kayla joked.

"Ha!" Agnes laughed out loud, caught by surprise at Kayla's boldness.

"Shhh Agnes! Some of us are trying to concentrate on tonight's event," Kayla sassily remarked.

Agnes pursed her lips and turned her focus upon the next guest entering the hall.

"Presenting Hyacinth, High Witch of the wendigast," Eshu continued.

"All hail Hyacinth," the crowd, especially the male members, chanted with more gusto.

"Greetings, peasants," the High Witch mocked as she made her entrance.

The ghouls around the handmaidens hissed at the insult, but refrained from rebelling any further. Agnes and Kayla gave each other a knowing look.

Hyacinth, the inspiration behind Agnes's plan for vengeance, took her seat to the Goddess's right. The long-limbed, gangly creature with cobwebs for hair, who was part witch, part tree-spirit, towered over the Goddess at her side. Her gown of plated bark was the traditional attire of her coven. The history books say that the bark gowns were designed to help ground the magically gifted race to nature. The witches were capable of not only elemental magic, but of using nature to brew potent magical herbal potions and remedies.

"That ridiculous gown makes the woman look more like a tree stump than a witch," Kayla snickered.

Agnes bit her lip to suppress a laugh, but nodded barely perceptively in agreement. Kayla smiled smugly at her side.

The wendigast preferred the taste and sustenance of human hearts, but any flesh would tide them over. The handmaiden recalled stories from her childhood of towns binding living human sacrifices to the edge of their surrounding forests. An offering to the witches in the hope that, during the coven's spiritual gatherings, they would spare the rest of the townsfolk from forming part of their meal.

"And finally, presenting his excellency, Ilbis, leader of the ghouls," Eshu proclaimed.

The ghouls cheered. Their raucous noise echoing off the walls, drowning out the welcoming proclamation of the rest of the crowd.

Kayla and Agnes looked at each other in alarm. They had known Ilbis would be here. Kayla had spread the gossip herself for goodness sake. But seeing was believing. And right now, they shared the same space as one of the most powerful and wicked creatures of all time. Agnes felt her body begin to tremble as she momentarily struggled to regain her composure.

"Hush, my children," Ilbis smoothly admonished as he entered the Hall of Bone, though he grinned in smug satisfaction.

Ilbis was the first of Nushka's creations; the crowning jewel of her achievements. Nearly as old as Moor itself. Ilbis, as with all the Goddess's allies, was born from her unholy magic and formed in the image of Nushka's deepest, darkest desires. He was her child of sorts. A nightmare made flesh.

The ground shook beneath the imposing monster's feet. Sheer power radiated off him, akin to that of his creator. His offspring, the ghouls, continued to cheer despite his mild reprimand.

Ilbis bore the gift of compulsion and manipulation. He could command anyone or anything to bend to his will. A gifting similar to Agnes's former mind conqueror powers, but far more potent. In contrast, her former gifting was like a drop in the ocean compared to what Ilbis could do.

The mortal realm was Ilbis's playground to conquer and wreak havoc upon as he saw fit. Were it not for the watchful eyes of Archè and Aria, he would have likely done just that in the immortal lands. He was a formidable and loyal ally to the Goddess who created him, yet how Nushka still held his reins she did not know. What a team Ilbis and Nushka would make together.

It was so rare to witness this many magical beings in Moor at any one time. Though any fool present still understood that, the Goddess of Blood and Bone was the most powerful of them all.

Once the Goddess's allies were in place, Nushka rose from her throne and Agnes felt herself inhale deeply through her useless lungs. The human habit was still as much a part of her as her wasted emotions. Kayla briefly squeezed her hand in reassurance. The show of kindness took Agnes by surprise.

"Welcome!" Nushka announced with sinister delight, showcasing her jagged teeth and dark power for all to see. Her shadows fleetingly flooded the room, burning away any trace of filth. A small demonstration of what she could do, a reminder for all to stay in line.

"Welcome to this historic gathering of allies. In Moor, wickedness is valued. Eternal torment and sinful pleasures are encouraged. Welcome to The Pitts of Moor. Welcome to my domain."

The Goddess of Blood and Bone

The Hall of Bone reeked of fear and primal need. Nushka inhaled deeply, turning the crowd's emotions into strength, her creations-turned-allies flanking her. The room was cramped, full of more allied forces than she had seen in an age. They squeezed between her chosen ones, the few souls she could stand to have in her presence.

"My wine!" The Goddess demanded, furious that she should have to ask for something that should have been readily given.

The Goddess's claws clicked against each other, promising violence. Her long midnight hair whipped around her waist impatiently.

Eshu approached the dais on unsteady knees, panic exuding from his every pore. He bowed, holding up the wine for the Queen with shaking hands.

"My apologies Your Majesty," he groveled, bowing incessantly. "Please forgive my insolence."

"Don't make me wait again or I will find a new mediator to the mortal realm," she warned. "Now get out of my sight."

The Goddess dismissed the mediator with a wave of her hand. She would likely have need of him in the days ahead, so she resisted the urge to eviscerate the messenger where he stood. After all, faithful underlings were in short supply, even if his loyalty was powered by fear and contempt.

The Goddess drew her attention back to her guests. Ilbis, her oldest and most powerful creation, had taken some convincing to attend the gathering. His endless pulling on her reins grew tiresome. The long leash she had granted him had turned him rebellious. Should he pull too hard, she would remind him exactly who was at the head of his food chain. Let him see how quickly his existence could be wiped from the universe, if he dared push her limits any further.

The Goddess of Blood and Bone found herself in a rare forgiving mood and decided not to smite Ilbis where he arrogantly stood. Instead, she faced her audience in a more amicable way than she or they were accustomed to.

It was when Nushka was at her most pleasant that her entrusted souls feared her the most… and rightfully so. *For what is dead cannot die*, but there are worse things imaginable.

'It is far easier to rule The Pitts as a beast than a woman,' Nushka mused.

She cleared her throat, raising a glass to those assembled.

"We are gathered here today for a purpose. Our common enemy, The Gods, binding us together," the Goddess resumed with a flash of her fangs. "Too long have we been confined to this realm. For too long have we held ourselves back from reaching our full wicked potentials. The time has come to take what is ours, and unleash ourselves upon the mortal and immortal realms. Far too long have we been confined to the shadows!" Nushka roared.

The crowd of souls cheered, her chosen ones and allies applauding, the chimera roaring in agreement. The hall became a cacophony of sound echoing off the freshly-cleaned bone walls. The Goddess straightened to her full height, drinking deeply from her glass of red wine and soaking up their bloodlust. As she absorbed the crowd's enthusiasm, turning their emanating energy into power, magic flooded through her veins, replenishing even the deepest depths of her being. Her shadows sung with renewed vigor. The soft glow of her porcelain skin shone even brighter.

Eshu rushed to the Goddess's side.

"You Majesty," he bowed, before replacing her empty glass with a filled chalice. The heady wine calling to her.

The Goddess ignored Eshu wholly as she took the glass. Then she flashed the crowd a wicked grin, her sharp teeth bared, her eyes simmering as she gazed upon her minions. Her veins sang with power as she consumed their energies. She let her power unfurl, shadows curling at her feet, reminding them who was Queen. Who ruled over all.

"We will bring the Land of the Gods to its knees!" Nushka declared.

Another raucous round of applause sounded, but the Goddess pushed on.

"Tonight, we celebrate! Tomorrow, we prepare for war. The Land of the Gods and the mortal realms are ours to conqueror! To victory!"

"To victory!" the hall echoed.

As the Goddess drank deeply, she noticed out of the corner of her eye, one of her handmaidens watching on with more eagerness than she was used to. Another of her handmaidens oddly by her side. A rare moment of curiosity took the Goddess by surprise, as Agnes tenaciously met her gaze. In her sheer black gown, looking sinfully tempting, she stepped boldly out from behind the ghouls that the pair had tried dismally to hide behind.

Leisurely drawing out each step, Agnes began a slow, seductive approach towards the dais. A devious smirk and glimmer in her eyes peaked the Goddess's interest. At Agnes's unrelenting gaze, Nushka felt her core tighten as heat pooled between her legs.

'*What is the hellcat up to now…*' Nushka pondered wickedly, the thrill of the unknown sending a delightful shiver down her spine.

"Agnes…" The Goddess remarked when her handmaiden finally arrived and bowed low at her feet.

"My Queen," Agnes warmly greeted her, fully aware of the Queen of Moor's rapt attention. "I have come to offer myself in service to you."

"Is that so…" Nushka contemplated, raking her eyes over the handmaiden before rising smoothly from her throne. "Follow me."

The Deity's near sentient hair momentarily fell limp at her waist. Behaving as if it were so overwhelmed by the myriad of conflicting thoughts and bodily reactions running through its master, it did not know how to react.

Agnes took her time rising from her position, licking her lips temptingly as she did so. Her delicate gown of flimsy fabric left little to the imagination. There was not an inch of Nushka's skin that Agnes had not explored, tasted. The thought sent goosebumps pebbling over her flesh.

"It would be an honor, My Queen," Agnes replied tenderly, her fingers curling around the ends of her hair.

Heat stirred in the Goddess's wicked core as she stood in place at the heart of the stage. Her surrounding allies sharing the dais were all but forgotten. Zeri, who had been comically curled at the Goddess's feet in the form of a cerberus, whimpered low in displeasure, sensing its master's impending exit.

Nushka smiled but tutted the beast. "Don't worry, Zeri, I will be back soon enough. Why don't you go and find some underling to maul while I'm gone?"

She patted each of his three heads before fluidly descending the back stairs of the dais, leaving her allies behind.

Her pet instantly calmed, each of his three heads licking their lips as they sized up the inhabitants in the room. The Queen's shadows trailed behind her with each graceful movement.

For reasons unknown, Nushka led the handmaiden not towards her usual suite, but deep into the heart of the bone castle. Levels below the surface, concealed by magical enchantments, awaited the Goddess's rose-scented candle-lit sanctuary.

The hot springs was a secluded, naturally heated pool; the only one of its kind beneath the Goddess's seat of power. A private hide-away of sorts that Nushka had allowed few allies to see and experience.

With a wave of Nushka's hand, Agnes morphed into corporal form, spirit made flesh. A rare gift for the Goddess to bestow upon one of her servants. A reward of sorts for pursuing her so brazenly.

"Shall we?" Nushka offered.

"As you wish, My Queen," Agnes answered with a reverent bow of her head.

☽ 5 ☾

The Goddess of Blood and Bone

The Queen of Moor sauntered towards the rocks bordering the springs, swishing her hips, her long serpentine hair moving gently in time. Her gown of liquid night flowed smoothly across her slender frame, accentuating every move and subtle curve. Her porcelain skin seemed to glow from within.

The Goddess of Blood and Bone stopped at the edge of the springs, the footsteps of her handmaiden trailing lightly behind her. Now that she was in corporal form, Nushka could smell the need pooling in her too. She could almost feel the moisture between her legs that she knew mirrored her own.

"I have been waiting for this day for a long time," Nushka professed. "The day that you would come crawling to me…"

"I am sorry to have kept you waiting, My Queen. But I am here now and I am all yours," Agnes offered in a sultry tone.

Nushka knew it was an act, but she was happy to play along... for now.

The Goddess knew Agnes was not always content to see to her needs. She was as strong-willed and stubborn as any Royal, but that was part of the draw for Nushka. Always wanting what she could never truly have. It made the game between them more enticing. Agnes never refused her though, had always agreed to whatever was demanded of her, always willing to satisfy any fantasy the Queen of Moor had dreamed up that night. Today, however, it appeared the handmaiden's own needs had outweighed her pride.

Agnes's forwardness and brazen disregard for her allies' presence during the revelry sent a thrill through her, heightening her voracious cravings for flesh and release.

"So, what makes today so special? What is it that you want?" Nushka asked icily.

"Can a servant not shower her Queen with the affection she deserves?" Agnes laid on thick.

Nushka huffed a laugh and rolled her eyes.

"The day you genuinely enjoy my company, and I yours, for that matter... Is the day The Pitts freeze over."

"Perhaps," Agnes winked, and Nushka couldn't help herself but she smiled.

Standing on the edge of a warm rock, Nushka retracted her claws and gently untied the ribbons that held her gown in place. A swathe of black silk pooled around her feet. Her midnight twisting hair and shadow magic her only adornments.

"I grow tired of all this talk, let's play," Nushka declared.

"As you wish, My Queen," Agnes agreed, giving her a sultry look.

Aware of her every movement and of the handmaiden behind her drinking in her bare skin and subtle curves, Nushka unhurriedly eased into the water. Her fluid movements akin to the peuchen. The pool's surface rippling across her chest. Her writhing shadow magic mingled gleefully with the steam of the hot springs, and the strong scent of rose from her candles filled the space.

Nushka remained facing away from her handmaiden as the sound of Agnes's gossamer gown met the floor. Breathing heavily, her heart raced in anticipation as the water lapped at her skin, while her servant entered the warm pool behind her.

Agnes halted a step away, her breath close enough to tickle Nushka's neck, but she did not dare advance any farther.

"How may I serve you My Queen?" Agnes asked huskily.

Ever so slowly, Nushka turned around to face the maiden. Deep, soulful brown eyes met her sharp emerald gaze. They were so close, the air between them taut. Agnes bit her bottom lip ever so slightly as she waited for Nushka to make the first move.

"I have a few ideas..." Nushka trailed off.

Beneath the water's surface, Nushka began tracing idle circles along the maiden's side with a feather-light touch. Allowing her claws to extend, she softly scraped along the side of the maiden's breast. Her skin felt as soft as velvet. Agnes inhaled sharply at her touch. Her breath catching. She took in her fill of Agnes's peaked breasts bared above the rippling water's surface.

With her other hand, Nushka gently took Agnes's left hand in her own and directed it to where she needed her the most. Her slick, sensitive skin singing at her touch.

"Perhaps you could start here…" Nushka suggested anything but innocently.

"Anything, to ensure your happiness My Queen…" Agnes simpered.

The first finger that teasingly stroked Nushka felt like blessed relief. Slowly, Agnes increased the pressure she applied, her wicked fingers dancing over that bundle of sensitive nerves before finally sliding ever so leisurely inside her. Exactly where she needed. Unhurriedly, she began moving her fingers in and out of her body in slow taunting strokes, like a cat playing with a mouse.

"I hope this it to your liking…" Agnes remarked coyly.

Nushka found herself unable to speak, consumed by the luxurious strokes of those wicked fingers.

Agnes chuckled, "I'm glad I please you so."

The Goddess's sense of need and urgency compounded within her; a growing flame slowly burning her from the inside out. This feeling was everything.

Nushka moved her left hand to cup and massage her servant's breast, her claws once more retracted. Taking, always taking what she wanted. Agnes's nipple hardened beneath her touch, much to the Goddess's gratification. Agnes released an involuntary moan at the rare pleasure she was receiving rather than administering. The moan sent electricity through Nushka as her lips found Agnes's. Their tongues forcefully answering each other's demands. Agnes brought her other hand up to grasp the Goddess's breast in return.

Agnes pulled her mouth away from Nushka, from the clash of teeth and tongues.

"I hope this pleases you My Queen," Agnes promised breathlessly before lowering her mouth to taste her Queen.

After taking in the fullness of her with her sinful mouth, Agnes's tongue flicked against the Goddess's hard nipple. Her teeth biting down ever so tauntingly. Nushka shuddered beneath her touch. She sucked and leisurely explored the Queen's breast, all the while her fingers continued her ministrations, drawing out the Goddess's pleasure.

Flicking her tongue over the Goddess's nipple once more, Nushka curved into her touch.

"More. Fuck, I need more…" Nushka whimpered.

And Agnes delivered.

The handmaiden redirected her fingers from teasing strokes to pulsing inside the Queen, harder and faster now. Nushka couldn't help herself as she began grinding against her handmaiden's fingers, fucking her, needing her deeper. She rode her, until her vision blurred from ecstasy.

Nushka cursed herself for craving this from the rabble. But that feeling, that tantalizing feeling, it transformed her immortal, mundane existence into something more. That feeling of living. Agnes's thumb began massaging her Queen in just the spot, whilst her tongue continued to tease her breast. Nushka released a primal moan she couldn't contain as they continued exploring each other, drawing out each other's pleasure.

Nushka edged her way back onto a rock on the side of the pool so that Agnes could fully tend to her. Her bare, unblemished skin like moonlight made flesh. Her long midnight hair frantically whipped behind her in response to the building tension within. She needed it *now*.

As the handmaiden continued her ministration with her clever little fingers, her mouth no longer exploring her breast, the Goddess spread her legs, silently demanding. Living. This was what it felt like to live, unbound by rules or time. Relishing the moment.

The Goddess moved her clawed hands to fist them amongst Agnes's long blonde locks as she re-directed her mouth to where she craved her the most.

"Your Queen has need of that filthy mouth elsewhere," she rasped.

Fire smoldered in Agnes's deep brown eyes. "Whatever you need My Queen, you shall have..." she promised.

As Agnes continued to pump her fingers inside the Queen, she lowered her head and caressed her tongue along the inside of Nushka's thigh. The Goddess arched into the handmaiden's touch, still riding her fingers like a beast. She craved more, needed more. Another moan escaped her lips as Agnes continued to tease her with that mischievous tongue of hers, those full luscious lips, before finally, finally answering her sinful demands and feasting upon her.

"Fucking hell," Nushka roared as the need grew stronger and stronger inside of her.

Each stroke of her handmaiden's tongue was the answer to some unholy prayer. Only this once had she treated Agnes even remotely like an equal, only this once had she placed herself in such a vulnerable position to an underling. The Goddess didn't know why today was different, and in that moment, she didn't fucking care. The thrill of it fueled her inner fire. Her dark desires beckoning for more, craving more. Her depraved soul sang in earnest.

Another moan escaped Nushka's lips. Agnes's returning muffled moan sent heat flooding through her.

The pressure within continued to build as the Goddess thrust in time with her handmaiden's pulsing fingers and tantalizing tongue. Writhing against her, she silently begged for more. Agnes answered. She replaced her fingers with her tongue and suddenly the Queen couldn't catch a breath.

The desire and longing for release all too quickly became agonizing. She didn't want to play anymore; she'd had enough of her handmaiden's teasing. The need building within her begged for release. The Goddess arched her back, tilting her pelvis to allow the maiden easier access to tend to her more deeply.

Nushka pleaded for more, as she fucked Agnes's mouth. She had never asked for anything in her life, except for this. Her hands fisted deeper into the handmaiden's hair.

Each breath rasped as contentment was drawn out of her. Agnes replaced her tongue once more with her fingers, working her sharply and deeply. Her tongue replaced her massaging thumb as she anticipated her Queen's needs.

Moments later, as release found the Goddess, she flung her head backwards, freeing Agnes's hair as she roared gloriously towards the castle above, her shadows blotting out all light before simmering down like a second skin. The pool and the ground trembled beneath the power she released as she found her climax.

Her alabaster skin glowed beneath the raging shadows. A warmth flooded through her, the pleasure so powerful, so satisfying, that she found her eyes fluttering closed, savoring the feeling.

Lowering her head after a moment, panting softly, the Queen eased back into the water before her maid and kissed her gently. The lingering release echoed with every taunting slow pulse of her maiden's fingers until at last her need was fully sated, and the handmaiden leisurely ceased her ministrations.

Drawing her mouth away from Agnes's lips, the Queen smirked.

"That was... unexpected," Nushka rasped, still trying to catch her breath.

"You're welcome My Queen," Agnes grinned wickedly, her breathing labored.

Sudden unease swelled in the Goddess's stomach. A feeling that stemmed from allowing herself to be vulnerable. A situation that she considered utterly abhorrent. To be vulnerable was to be weak and she was not weak.

Nushka came to her senses and with a wave of her hand Agnes was once more in spirit form. A dismissive move by the Goddess to remind her servant who was in control here, despite Nushka enjoying her company.

"Lest you forget your place..." Nushka snarled taking a step back.

Nushka did not miss the flash of disappointment that crossed Agnes's face. A fact that gave the Goddess a different kind of gratification. The kind of enjoyment that came from delighting in the disappointment and pain of others. Satisfaction from causing heartache. A small part of her questioned if she had acted too brashly, but the wise part of her knew that the handmaiden meant nothing and she needed to reassert her dominance. And if that train of thought made her the nastiest immortal alive, she didn't give a fuck.

"I hope I have pleased you, My Queen," Agnes remarked insincerely, nostrils flaring.

Even in soul form, Agnes's now sullen brown eyes exuded dejection.

"You have served your Goddess well. But this was just sex, nothing more," Nushka glowered. "Count yourself fortunate that your Queen allowed you to enjoy the privilege of her own ministrations. It will not happen again. You are a servant and nothing more. One pleasant evening does not mean my feelings for you have changed. You are a worthless handmaiden and I am a Deity. You mean nothing to me," the Goddess of Blood and Bone spat, flexing her claws for emphasis.

Agnes straightened at her tone, and a flash of rage crossed her face at the dismissal, just as the Goddess liked it. Order once more restored.

"Now leave me," Nushka snapped. "And do not approach me again unless you are summonsed."

Agnes stood there momentarily dumbfounded.

The Goddess exited the pool with impossible grace and stood once more upon the rocks, completely bare. With little effort, her power had her dry and redressed in her gown. Her hair calmly swayed at her back, clinging to the endorphins still flooding the Goddess's very being. Her shadows pooled around her.

Head bowed, Agnes exited the pool in soul form and as she did so, her flimsy black gown reappeared upon her frame. She paused for a moment, then bit her lip as if weighing her words. To dare challenge the Goddess now, she must know, would be a permanent death sentence despite gaining the Goddess's favor.

"My Queen," Agnes spoke hesitantly. "There is something I wish to discuss with you."

Nushka stared at her in disbelief which quickly gave way to rage.

"Ha! The reason for your offering I suspect!" Nushka's tone cold and unrelenting. "In case you didn't hear me the first time, I told you to get the fuck out of my sight! Do you want me to end your existence?" Nushka thundered.

Agnes bravely raised her head, eyes burning with conviction. Nushka caught a glimpse of the calculating warrior within.

"I can help you take over the Land of the Gods," Agnes announced. "I have a plan to do it, and it does not require a war."

Agnes

Hands fisted, teeth clenched, Agnes tried desperately to subdue the bottomless pit of rage that welled within. To cast her aside like that, to return her to her spirit form, even when the Goddess had so obviously enjoyed herself, was cold, even for her. To treat her with such disrespect...

Now, as the Queen of Moor led them towards the War Chamber, it took all of Agnes's might to not scream her frustration at the Deity. To fight Nushka on this would only make life harder for herself—might cost her everything. She tried and failed to rein in her anger, her frazzled thoughts clouding her better judgement.

Caught up in the passion of the moment they shared in the pool, Agnes had dared consider that she might have meant something to the Goddess. How wrong she had been to think for even a second that Nushka could possibly care for anyone other than herself. It was just sex for the Deity. She had made that perfectly clear.

'I will never allow myself to become as heartless as her. I will never give up that speck of humanity within me, that prevents my human soul from giving way to the beast within. There must be a better way to live. I want more than this pitiful existence.'

With a heavy sigh, Agnes pushed her thoughts and feelings aside, needing to refocus on the plan and her end game.

As Agnes had beheld Hyacinth, the High Witch of the wendigast that evening, she had known exactly what she needed to do. Thus, a variation of the original plan began to form in her mind. A plan still inspired by Hyacinth's rise to power, but one that played more to her strengths. If all went well, the Queen of Moor would be indebted to her. A way of shifting the balance of power between them forevermore, not just temporarily in the bedroom. A way to secure her eternal existence, and attain an afterlife worth living.

Agnes and the Goddess of Blood and Bone approached the entrance to the War Chamber, the latter's shadows writhing. Two peuchen guarding the entrance slithered away from the double doors to permit them access. The peuchen were smaller than usual, likely still young, though they still filled much of the hall. They left only a couple of feet between them for the Deity and handmaiden to walk between. Their black scales glimmered in the light reflected off the lit sconces lining the hall.

Without a word, the Goddess glided through the double bone doors and took her place upon the imposing stone chair at the head of the table. The War Chamber was exactly how Agnes had imagined it; a smaller version of the throne room with soaring bone walls, a long rectangular table made of volcanic rock and an assortment of chairs to accommodate various creatures' shapes and sizes. Two burning hearths either side of the room provided the only source of light in the windowless chamber.

Agnes gently closed the bone doors behind them before approaching the long table, head held high. Clouds of shadow radiated irately off the Dark Queen.

"Sit," Nushka commanded, and Agnes did as she was told, taking a seat two places down from the Queen, keeping a respectful and wise distance away.

The Goddess's hair whipped frantically around her. Her eyes blazing, Nushka surveyed Agnes with a look of utter contempt.

"You may present your plan but choose your words carefully. If you waste my time, I will end yours," The Goddess reckoned.

A sinister smirk adorned the Deity's face as she scratched her claws against the table, the sound akin to screeches on a blackboard. Agnes knew that look well. It promised pain should one displease the Queen.

Self-preservation finally allowed her to see better sense, as she set aside the remnants of her anger to focus on the task at hand. Agnes straightened in the hard stone chair and spoke frankly.

"My family are living the life of luxury either in the Land of Milk and Honey, or alive and well in Alearia," Agnes explained before she lost her nerve. "I want the vengeance that is owed to me. I want to make all the do-gooders pay from treating us *other-minded* souls as less than worthy. Everyone loves a hero, but being a villain is far more compelling. Besides, the only thing that separates the moral from the immoral, is that villains are not afraid to defy social norms. Villains will do whatever it takes to achieve their end game, and I will do whatever it takes to make you Ruler of the Gods," Agnes divulged.

"How are *you*, a *worthless*, insignificant handmaiden, going to help *me* defeat the Gods? A task that in all my existence I have thus far failed to do. Do not insult me by insinuating that you are more cunning than I," Nushka reprimanded, leaning forward on the table, staring daggers towards the maid.

The Goddess's spiteful words found their mark, but Agnes did not give her the satisfaction of letting it show. Instead, the handmaiden kept her head held high and took a deep breath—a now useless trick from her human days—and refocused. The act of deep breathing still helped, even if breathing was no longer a necessity in spirit form.

"From a young age," Agnes began, "I was trained to say and do all the right things, to disguise my true intentions. I learned all the courtly, manipulative tricks. Lies and deceptions passed my lips so smoothly that I could deceive even my own family with little effort. That is how I know, without a doubt, that I can fool Archè himself. Together, we will invoke the rule of redemption," Agnes smugly proclaimed.

The Goddess appraised her momentarily, before gesturing with a noncommittal flourish of her clawed hand for the handmaiden to continue. Agnes knew the wicked Queen would grow tired of her before long, that she was living on borrowed time, but she had somehow caught the Goddess's mild curiosity and so she would make every word count.

"Offer me up for the Goddess of Darkness's re-appraisal," Agnes continued desperately. "If I can convince Lilith that I am redeemed and worthy of the Afterworld, then Archè will offer you a place in the Land of the Gods once more. I heard about the rule of redemption in Moor. I know we can do this."

Nushka looked at her as if she had utterly lost her mind. Perhaps she had, but she was not going to give up. Agnes knew that she could do it, that all her training had led to this. A chance to enact revenge.

"We will re-enact the story of Hyacinth's rise," Agnes continued urgently. She grappled to hold the Queen's attention and avoid becoming the late-night amusement in the castle's torture chambers. "After I am welcomed into the Land of the Gods, my soul considered redeemed by Lilith, they will surely hold a banquet or ball in your honor to welcome you back into the fold. Before the event, I will slip a tonic prepared by Hyacinth herself into their drinks, rendering the Gods powerless. I will pave the way for you to sweep in with your allies and take what is rightfully yours. Only then will you be free to obtain your vengeance, to destroy Archè and Aria, and take your place as Queen of the Gods."

Agnes sank into her chair, feeling the Goddess's penetrating stare rake over her, weighing the merit of her words. Agnes prayed she had not overstepped and doomed herself to pain for her insolence.

"My sister, Lilith, is ruthless. She and I are one and the same in so many ways. What makes you think you could outsmart her? What makes you think that, after a millennium of attempting to have souls re-appraised, you will be any different?" Nushka raised an eyebrow.

Agnes leaned forward and spoke with the voice of a Queen.

"I want power and I will do whatever it takes to get it. If I can convince you that I can do this, then I stand a good chance at convincing Lilith that I am a changed woman," Agnes assured her.

"If I fail, then you are no worse off. But if you start a war without trying my idea first, you could stand to lose countless followers and allies in an all-out war with the Gods that you may not even win. We can prevent numerous deaths and guarantee success with my plan. It's possible to take the ultimate seat of power through scheming rather than violence, I know it is."

"I suppose you believe you are entitled to something in return for your assistance?" Nushka speculated. Her shadows furled and unfurled ready to strike.

Agnes tilted her chin, brazen defiance written on her face.

"I want you to restore my life force, transform me into an immortal and restore my former mind conqueror gifting. After that is done, I want command over the Afterworld."

The handmaiden's spirit quivered as she walked a dangerous line with the Goddess, a being who could destroy her with a mere thought. Nushka rose from her chair and moved to open the bone door back out to the hallway.

Turning on her heels to face Agnes directly, Nushka demanded: "Why should I reward you for something I could simply order you to do? I am a Deity after all, and you are nothing more than a servant whose company I am quickly growing tired of."

Agnes raised her chin boldly, drawing on her last dregs of courage.

"You need me," she said fearlessly, looking down her nose at the Queen. "If you do not agree to my terms, I will tell Lilith of your plans to overthrow the Land of the Gods. Before you even have a chance to rally your allied forces. Archè himself will arrive and smite you where you stand. And before you act brashly, you should know that I have briefed someone in The Pitts to send a message to Lilith if I am wiped from existence during this meeting."

Off course that wasn't true, but Nushka didn't know that. Agnes silently prayed the Goddess didn't see through her deceit.

"Alternatively," Agnes continued more confidently, "if you deny me the chance to prove myself to Lilith, you will risk losing countless allies in a war you cannot win. Not if the Gods retain their powers. So, I suggest you let me help you and reward me as I deserve."

A smirk grew across the Goddess's pale face.

"Fine," Nushka replied indifferently. "We will try it your way. But if you fail, I will roast you, torture you and place your corporal head on a spike. After all that is done, I will banish you to the ether for all eternity. Do we have an accord?"

Agnes gulped, or she would have if her body were once more corporal. She rose from her chair and followed the Goddess's cue of dismissal.

"As you wish, My Queen," she agreed, bowing unsteadily.

Agnes quickly made for the door.

"Just one more thing Agnes..." Nushka added, stopping her in her tracks.

Agnes cautiously faced the Deity.

"Yes, My Queen," her voice shuddered.

"You will find it is not in your best interests to attempt to blackmail a Goddess. I will allow you to leave this room safely but I will not be so merciful the next time you cross me," she cautioned.

"Thank you My Queen."

The handmaiden did not notice the peuchen's overbearing presence as she hurriedly exited the War Chamber. Not as the Goddess slammed the door after her, a tremor of shadow power reverberating into the hallway. Agnes did not dare look back as she quickened her pace, trying to create as much distance between her the Deity. The Queen likely dreaming of wiping the floor with her bloody corpse.

Agnes

Her freedom was short lived, as Agnes found herself unceremoniously thrown into the dark, rancid cell beneath the bone castle. The two peuchen that had guarded the War Chamber were not gentle by any means as they wrapped their tails around her newly returned corporal form, constricting around her waist, before dumping her on the hard-slate dungeon floor. Agnes figured the peuchen had received the order telepathically. A useful gift for guards, she mused. It would also appear that the Goddess of Blood and Bone did not even need to be in proximity to change Agnes's form. A piece of information that may prove useful later.

Daring to blackmail and then make demands of the Goddess was never wise, Agnes knew that. But desperate times had called for drastic measures. She wouldn't continue existing the way she had these past five years, couldn't bear the thought of it. She had needed to act, even if it meant stooping to the Goddess's level.

She regretted nothing and would do it all again knowing her actions had achieved the desired outcome.

Agnes counted herself lucky that the Goddess had not decided to punish her by wiping her from all existence or worse, torturing her. Confining Agnes to a cell was the Goddess's way of restoring the hierarchy of power. A means of reminding the handmaiden of who exactly she served and what she was to the Goddess—nothing—despite the intimate moment they had shared.

Agnes was not unfamiliar with imprisonment. She recalled long days spent in the Castle Brandistone dungeon as she awaited her death sentence to be carried out. Her crimes against the crown and Kingdom of Alearia deemed unforgivable even from a Royal. She had been lucky then, to have escaped. Her pathetic, soft-hearted sisters had helped her break out. Weak. They had always been weaker than her, even stubborn as hell Alecia. This time, however, was the first time she had received such treatment since passing into the afterlife.

"Same fucking shit, different realm," Agnes muttered.

Cobwebs, dried blood, and all manner of filth clung to the grimy bone walls and low ceiling. The cell had likely not been cleaned in centuries, if at all. Previous prisoners had etched their names into the bones, ensuring that somewhere their names lived on, even if they did not. Those deprived of an eternal existence, she mused, were still more fortunate than most in The Pitts. To suffer an infinity of pain and torture in Moor, was an eternity that made even Agnes's dark heart cringe. Perhaps it was her fate, yet somehow, she didn't think so.

Truth be told, the likely short stay in the cell was a welcome reprieve from her regular duties as a handmaiden. Even if the surrounds were pitiful accommodation for a former Royal. However, an opportunity to plan her vengeance alone in silence was a rare chance indeed.

In fact, compared to her usual experience of existing in The Pitts of Moor, having a space to herself, no matter how decrepit, felt like an unintentional reward masked as punishment.

"How far I have fallen, to consider this hell hole a reward." Agnes rolled her eyes as she slumped down on the rough hay bed on the far side of the cell. The only luxury that the Goddess had allowed in her eight-foot by eight-foot cell. The feel of the itchy straw on her skin was surprisingly welcome after being deprived of physical senses for too long in her spirit form.

"How fucking far I have fallen indeed," she cursed into the darkness.

It was rare for the Goddess to allow the fallen the privilege of returning to their corporal form, even in the bedroom. Instead, magic allowed the Goddess to feel each of her handmaiden's ministrations without their bodies being fully present. Nushka rarely gave, only received or seized what she believed was her Goddess-given right. It had likely seemed pointless to her, for her handmaidens to enjoy the same experience.

'How strange it feels to be back in my human form for so long. Even if its sole reasoning is to keep me confined to this wretched cell. But my stay here will be short. Nushka needs me if she wishes to take over the Land of the Gods. In aiding her, I will finally obtain a seat of unchallenged power.'

Seeing to Nushka's *desires* today in her physical form had altered the balance between them, no matter that it was only for a moment. But in that brief moment, Agnes had felt like she had mattered. She cursed herself for being so stupid and offering herself so freely to the Goddess who had discarded her like old news. Her existence held no value to Nushka and that would never change. She reminded herself that she was no-one's whore and, after this was all over with, Agnes would make the Goddess pay for treating her as such.

It vexed Agnes to admit to herself that, after being starved of genuine physical contact for so long, the Goddess's returning touch had felt electric. As if her very being felt alive again. Even the warm water rippling over her skin had felt sensual. Between her legs, despite her hatred of the Goddess, heat pooled within her at the recollection of Nushka's hand caressing her breast. The taste of

Nushka upon her lips had satisfied her in a way that she had not experienced in such a long time.

Despite her circumstances and the unsterile conditions, Agnes found herself snatching up the rare opportunity to see to her own needs for a change. Too long had she waited to feel the intense physical pleasures that could only be experienced in corporal form. She would not be denied any longer. Alone, for the first time in what felt like an eternity, Agnes took advantage of the rare privacy and treated herself.

As her fingers danced beneath her sheer dress, she felt them moisten at the thought of stolen moments in the garden with Sir Riley back in Alearia. Of nights when they would melt into the shadows of the palace rose gardens and discover what made each other moan. Sometimes, they would sneak up to her bedchamber during a ball and find their pleasure beneath the sheets or against a wall.

Agnes had never cared for the noble, despite what he and her family thought. But he was easy on the eye, and the sex was like nothing she had ever experienced. Riley knew exactly how to please her. He knew exactly which places to tease to make her squirm, eliciting uncontrollable moans from her with each joining. The length of him had fit so perfectly inside of her, each tight pulse of him an agonizing relief.

Despite how phenomenal the sex had been, fucking him had been nothing more than a way of satisfying her own needs. Much as she pondered how the Goddess used her. There was not an inch of her that the noble had not explored with his tongue, had not tasted, or she of him. Incredibly handsome, but gullible as the village idiot. Sir Riley had served his purpose well.

Agnes thought of all their forbidden encounters as her need grew stronger. Her breathing deepened as she plummeted her slick fingers in and out, hard and deep, writhing beneath her own touch, desperate for release. Agnes quickened her pace rather than savoring each movement, eager for the destination, rather than the journey for dread of interruption. Teasing that bundle of nerves with her thumb; massaging herself in just the spot she liked it. Each moment was pure bliss.

After years of never having her thirst truly sated, Agnes relished in the undiluted pleasure of her physical touch, tending to her needs exactly how she liked it. A man beneath her, in this form, was what she craved more than anything, but to reach a culmination in corporal form by any means was all she needed. She was not going to let anything fuck this moment up.

Her fingers dried as her pace increased, so she drew those same fingers into her mouth to moisten them before continuing to draw out her pleasure. Rolling her thumb around the spot that undeniably brought her the greatest thrill. Agnes indulged in every wave of bliss that washed through her until, much sooner than she had expected, she found her climax. A pleasurable burn flowed over her body as she found her release. Agnes promised herself that before the Goddess deprived her of her physical form again, she would reach her pleasure once more.

The Goddess of Darkness

The moon was rising over Alearia in the clouded vision of the mortal realm that Lilith, the Goddess of Darkness, observed. Her long legs draped over the arm of her throne of sinners' souls encased in bone; the place she sentenced all those who deserved perpetuity in limbo. The hundreds of thousands of wretched souls trapped within her seat of power could only watch eternity slip by as the realms full of life whirled around them. Never able to exist in any way that held value, their souls slowly breaking down until they ceased to exist at all. The alternative to being sent to The Pitts of Moor or the Afterworld.

Only a handful of recently departed souls silently awaited their final judgement in the Hall of Shadows. A dark mist floating gently over the floor shrouded their translucent feet. All had met their demise from old age or disease, nothing exciting enough to draw Lilith's attention. Though the Goddess knew sometime soon she would need to deliver judgment upon their eternal souls. Most would likely be escorted through the Gates of the Afterworld, one or two might not.

Alearia was but one of the Kingdoms under the Goddess's charge. In the vision she now oversaw of the present, twin Princesses played hide-and-seek amongst the rose bushes in their family's private gardens. How innocent and carefree they seemed. Their mother, the Alearian Queen, her belly round with unborn child, pretended she couldn't hear her daughters' excitable giggles as she searched for them.

'How blissfully naïve they are,' the Goddess thought.

One day the twins will transform from best friends into bitter rivals in the often-brutal Crowning Ceremony rituals. Not just competing against each other, but against all their Davis-Brandistone royal siblings. Just as their mother Anastasia did before them.

The Crowning Ceremony tradition was created to determine the future Ruler of their Kingdom. A vicious cycle of sibling rivalry that continued generation after generation, pinning each sibling against each other in a power struggle. A tradition that brought the Goddess great joy as the antics unfolded. It was a blessed relief from the monotony of overseeing her Kingdoms through times of peace. A brutal but effective way of sorting out the weak from the strong, ensuring the future Ruler was fit to take over the empire when the time came. Lilith had held great hopes from the now reigning Queen's twin, but it was not to be.

The royal bloodlines from Shadows Peak and Alearia had since merged to produce four—soon to be five—magically gifted siblings. Their unleashed giftings would be a sight to behold in the next Crowing Ceremony events. Such strength that had not been witnessed in a mortal in centuries, exempting their Aunt Annalyse. Her mind conqueror gifting had rivaled the power of an immortal, but alas, her time had come to a premature end.

'A waste of such potential,' the Goddess thought disappointedly.

Yet the strength of the present Alearian Heirs' giftings were unparalleled by all other Royal Heirs in the many Kingdoms. The Goddess of Darkness had many plans for them. Lilith just hoped they would not prove to be as disappointing as their overly sweet mother. Her potential was squandered in the eyes of the Goddess, by her sanctimonious morals and ethics.

Lilith had watched her people flourish in recent years. It felt like only yesterday that Alearia had faced its last attempted invasion. The day her realm had changed for the better. The day a Kingdom was reminded of its fragility and began seeking their Goddess's guidance through prayer and worship once again.

'A pity that Annie, who I spent so much time and effort into shaping, was not able to see Alearia achieve peace. What a waste! At any rate, she served her purpose. Such a dull and soft-hearted soul is surely basking in her now unending existence in the Afterworld. Reunited with her absurdly sweet mentor and mother,' Lilith considered.

Lilith gazed into the handheld mirror she kept by her throne, and scoffed at the face that stared back at her. She released an exasperated sigh. The mortals' prayer and worship had declined of late, her people opting to instead devote the pleasant summer months to spending time with their friends and family. Their Goddess had become an afterthought.

'Ungrateful sycophants, only praying when it suits their own needs.'

Thus, her skin had begun to age once more, and her strength was waning. Even the shadow magic that rippled off her lacked its usual robustness, sluggishly lingering at the foot of the throne, as though it no longer possessed the strength to explore and seek out its prey.

For the first time since the battle for Alearia, much to Lilith's disgust, wrinkles had appeared beneath her eyes, her face more drawn than usual. A middle-aged woman stared back at her, rather than the youthful Deity she had been in times of war and throughout winter. It was on those occasions that her people remembered who they had to thank for their prosperity and who could take it away just as easily.

'Perhaps a friendly reminder of who holds power over them is in order,' Lilith mused as she threaded her long boney fingers through her black lusterless tresses.

A single curl of the Goddess's ebony hair fell away into her lap, causing Lilith to grimace. It was considered a great disgrace amongst the Gods for her power to have become so diminished that it affected her physical features. In a momentary fit of rage, she flung the age-old mirror across the hall, the glass shattering into a million pieces.

"Ungrateful humans!" she cursed.

The Goddess of Blood and Bone

This evening marked the first time the Goddess had left Moor in over a century. Nushka had given up hope of convincing Lilith that she could legitimately reform one of her entrusted souls. Nushka had never held any desire for goodness. She certainly did not know how to replicate the trait in others. However, lying, betrayal and vengeance were qualities she knew well. They were talents she had eons of experience honing into a fine art. Perhaps that made this new plan more likely to succeed. A scheme rooted in dishonesty rather than integrity.

Nushka had always preferred her older sister Lilith to her other siblings. Chiara, the Goddess of Light, was sickeningly honorable and grinded on Nushka's every nerve. Chiara's appointment as overseer of the Afterworld was the perfect place for the do-gooder to reign. Thorn, the God of War, who had always been closer to Lilith, had shown little interest in getting to know

Nushka. Thorn was all muscles and no brains as far as she was concerned. Lilith, however, she could relate to.

In terms of their appearance, Lilith and Nushka were remarkably similar. In terms of their natures, they both shared the same shadow magic and were more closely akin than any other Gods. However, where Nushka's heart was wicked to the core, Lilith's was far less repulsive.

The Goddess of Darkness was strangely curious about her human *pets*. She had been that way for as long as Nushka could remember. Lilith had even gone so far as to show an interest in the wellbeing of her worshippers. It was that compassion that Lilith showed towards the humans of her realms that Nushka perceived as weakness. The idea of forming any kind of attachment with your followers was abhorrent to the Goddess of Blood and Bone— unfathomable. The issue had been the cause of many a row between the sisters over the years. Thankfully, the Goddess of Darkness also had a practical side that Nushka could relate to. Lilith, unlike their other siblings, was not ruled by her feelings.

Deeming it easier to seek forgiveness than ask permission, Nushka transported herself unannounced into Lilith's domain. Claws extended, her shadows poised to strike, Nushka landed at the foot of the all too familiar dais.

Nushka inhaled the crisp, clean air of the Hall of Shadows. She had not noticed before; how different the atmosphere felt between their realms. Her senses had become smothered in Moor, and standing here, in a place free of contaminated air, she could breathe for what felt like the first time. The same spirits, the same slate floor, even a familiar bone throne was before her, so like home. But the air, the absence of the bone walls and the strange, unsettling sense of *peace* surprised her.

"Welcome, sister," Lilith spoke monotonously, her brow quirked.

Where Nushka moved with the fluidity of a serpent, Lilith had the grace of a dancer, perpetually floating on a cloud. As the Goddess of Darkness elegantly descended the dais stairs, Nushka could not help but take in her appearance.

"It has been an age, Lilith, since I have seen you looking so pathetic," Nushka playfully taunted, fully aware that she herself had never looked better. In Moor, surrounded by an endless amount of fearful souls she could draw strength from, Nushka appeared perpetually in her prime. Her physical appearance never suffered from lack of strength.

"I don't see how my appearance is any of your business. I'm surprised you aren't too blinded by your own ego to take notice," Lilith quipped.

Nushka tilted her head to the side, assessing her sister with snake-like emerald eyes. She took in Lilith's age lines, thinning hair, and the lack of spark in her trailing shadows and her lip curled in disgust.

"Do your pets no longer show you the proper respect that you deserve? Disgraceful, absolutely disgraceful."

Nushka straightened herself, crossing her arms, painted claws extended. The shadows at her feet danced, ready to pounce should her sister decide to bite back.

Lilith shrugged a shoulder, releasing a small sigh.

"Such a pleasure as always, Nushka. I see the years banished to The Pitts have not dampened your spirits," Lilith observed, her tone dripping with sarcasm.

Nushka grinned wickedly, her hair swaying eagerly.

"Ahh sister... you seem so thrilled to have me visit. I'm so glad! It has been far too long since we have sparred like this," Nushka heckled her sister.

"Well this happy reunion can wait another century or two. I have work to do," Lilith asserted, gesturing with a flourish of her arm towards the souls awaiting her judgement. "Say whatever it is you have come to say and then leave," she added.

Ignoring her sister's sinister grin, Lilith approached the first of the departed souls awaiting her judgement. The deceased was a thin elderly man, likely a farmer hailing from Alearia or Quillencia, based on his callused hands, weathered clothes, and slouched posture. Even in death, he did not look afraid of hard work. The farmer fell to his knees before the Goddess of Darkness, pitifully beseeching her for forgiveness for his past sins. He offered his praises, *begging* the Goddess to be reunited with his family in the Afterworld. Nushka did not miss the renewed vigor of Lilith's shadows as she no doubt absorbed his groveling. It barely counted as worship. A small smirk graced Nushka's lips at the sign that her earlier words had found their mark.

Ignoring her sister wholly now, Lilith placed a hand on the soul's shoulder, judging his worthiness with her gift of discernment. There was no dramatic magic in her gift, no physical manifestation for an onlooker to observe. The only indication of her completing her judgment was the withdrawal of her hand.

"Rise, Alfred," Lilith spoke solemnly. "You have served your family and Kingdom well. You will be rewarded for your lifetime of service. I will grant you safe passage through the Gates to the Afterworld."

Relief shone through the old man's eyes, much to the Goddess of Blood and Bone's distaste. All this pageantry grew tiring quickly.

"Get on with it, sister," Nushka demanded. "We have matters to discuss." Her lashed impatiently around her feet and dug its claws in a nearby awaiting soul. Luckily for the victim they were protected from pain whilst they remained in Lilith's realm.

Lilith glowered at her. "I told you to say your piece and then get out. So, do it!" she spat. "My work does not stop because you decide to grace me with your presence."

Nostrils flaring, lips pursed, Nushka struggled to keep a leash on her temper. Shadows danced in annoyance around the train of Lilith's midnight gown. So similar they were, Nushka noted to herself. So unlike the others.

When Lilith did not receive a response, she turned on her heels and escorted the man through the Gate to the Afterworld. For the few moments Lilith was gone, Nushka took the opportunity to better survey the Hall of Shadows. Less than a dozen souls awaited their eternal judgment, but more would come. Day by day, year by year, this was the life the Goddess of Darkness was *dictated* to *live*.

'*How different our eternal lives are,*' Nushka mused. '*In The Pitts, at least I have my minions to amuse me. I am not alone. I am not deprived of flesh or company. How wretched and lonely her existence must be. I could not exist like this. We have both been treated as less than we are; banished to rule over loathsome realms. All because Archè and Aria declare it to be so. Dictators from the beginning of time, pampered by their followers, unquestioned.*'

Nushka's hair twitched in irritation, her claws extending, shadows stirring as her temper built.

'Soon, their time will come, and Deities like my sister and I will not be treated as lesser. No longer will we be denied our rightful places amongst the Gods. Royal blood and unending power flood through our veins. We are Queens in our own rights, who have been treated like servants, like lesser Gods. This cannot continue.'

In a moment of frustration, seeking release from the anger burning within, she slashed a clawed hand across an awaiting soul's face. The movement startled the departed spirit but caused her no harm. Nushka internally cursed that the spirits in the hall were immune to her *gift* of pain.

A flash of light in the corner of her eye drew Nushka from her tumultuous thoughts, as Lilith returned to the Hall of Shadows through another portal that immediately closed behind her. Instead of attending to her next charge, Lilith gracefully returned to her throne of sinners' souls. Perched on the edge of her seat, straight-backed, she folded her hands neatly in her lap. A Queen ready to hold court.

"Why are you here Nushka?" Lilith demanded.

Nushka raised her chin defiantly from the foot of the dais, choking down distaste that rose from the unfamiliar need to request something from an equal. The Goddess of Blood and Bone only ever took what was hers, she did not make *requests*.

"I need you to re-appraise a soul entrusted into my care," Nushka requested with fierce determination. Her shadows billowed around her. Her hair flicked about frantically, sensing the rise in adrenaline flooding its master's body. "I wish to invoke the rule of redemption."

Lilith appraised her sister for a long moment, her face a blank mask. Just when Nushka was ready to give up, sure that her sister would soon laugh in her face, to her surprise the Goddess of Darkness nodded her head in agreement.

"Very well," Lilith said decisively, fire burning in her eyes. "Bring them to me."

Agnes

The days were long beneath the bone castle. Time measured only by the number of candles Agnes burned through to keep the darkness at bay. Each candle lasting only a handful of hours, she had to be quick to relight one off the other before it burnt out or else be left in darkness. Twenty-two pillar candles and counting. Occasional screams from neighboring cells broke the silence. The putrid scent of refuse and copper tang of blood only worsened, nausea surging in the handmaiden's stomach.

The novelty of being back in physical form had quickly worn thin. The former Royal's body fell prey to the harsh conditions of her confinement. Even though it was impossible for Agnes to die, as she was already technically dead, sensations and ailments still plagued her in this form. She had forgotten how cumbersome and fragile her mortal body had been. The illusion of pain in spirit form now seemed trivial compared to the real thing.

Painful blisters formed beneath Agnes's feet as the heat from the volcanic plains rose through the ground, like perpetually walking along hot coals. The stifling air and overpowering stench caused her to frequently gag. No longer did the handmaiden revel in the pleasurable side of her physical form. Pain and disgust were now front and center of her thoughts. Living in this cell, enduring this endless hell hole… this was a reminder from her Queen of what her life in Moor could have entailed, had she not earned the Goddess's favor.

The Dark Queen had not visited her prisoner, nor had she sent word regarding updates on Agnes's plan. Nushka had, however, arranged for Eshu, her mediator between the human realm and the Gods', to deliver her a gift. The Orb of Historia contained the history of the Gods since the beginning of time, a record-keeping relic that had been created by the first Gods. How Nushka had come into possession of the prized artifact, Agnes didn't know. Such a precious relic, ever-learning and adding to its wealth of knowledge, would have been coveted amongst the Gods. The fact the Goddess of Blood and Bone trusted her to use it was the only sign she would show that their tentative alliance still held.

Clouded visions appeared in the orb. The vessel's contents were endless, recounting historic events, maps, paintings, and ancient texts. If it was considered important to the Gods, then it could be found within the orb. Star charts for constellations and visions of galaxies that Agnes didn't even know existed, were all contained within its endless scope of information. Agnes marveled at the clarity and vibrant colors of a galactic scene, having never seen anything like it. The technology was so far advanced from her experience in the mortal realm that its vast knowledge was unfathomable. The bearer had merely to hold the object and envision the information they wished revealed before the vessel briefly hummed, and the requested piece of history would appear through the transparent glass.

Feet outstretched before her, wounds wrapped in water-soaked thread-bare linen strips torn from her gown, Agnes scrolled through the contents of the orb. The longer she suffered, the more she felt driven by anger to learn all she could, to help her bring the bastards down that pulled upon all her strings.

Deceiving the Goddess of Darkness was but the first part of her task. Navigating around the Land of the Gods, mingling amongst its Deities and finding a way to contaminate their drinking supply would be her next undertaking. Just as Hyacinth had done so eons ago to achieve her ends, Agnes would find a way too.

To get close enough to contaminate the drinking supply that would bring down the Gods, Agnes would first need to know her enemy. She required every advantage for her plan to succeed and would only have one chance. The former Royal shuddered to think of what would happen to her if she were discovered by Archè himself, for there were far worse things than being wiped away from all eternity.

"Agnes, are you in there?" a familiar voice whispered from the other side of the bone cell door drawing her from her thoughts.

Relief filled Agnes's chest.

She lowered the orb and hobbled over to the door, each painful step drawing a whimper from her.

"I'm here," she called as she stopped to rest against the wall beside the door.

"Thank the Gods," Kayla sighed as she walked through the bone door in spirit form.

Concern filled the handmaiden's semi-translucent face.

"Oh Agnes, are you okay?" she fretted. "I have been worried about you."

"You have?" Agnes straightened in disbelief.

"Of course," Kayla responded incredulously. "I know we are not friends, but that doesn't mean I don't care what happens to you. Besides, we have all suffered Nushka's wrath far worse in your absence. What in the realm did you do to end up in here?"

Something akin to guilt pooled in her stomach. Agnes had been so quick to assume that Kayla's positivity and kindness was all just an act, that she hadn't ever considered the possibility that she could be an even slightly decent person.

Despite the pain, Agnes smiled.

"It's a long story… But thank you for coming to check on me," she replied and meant it.

"Don't be silly. We handmaidens should look out for each other more often," Kayla remarked wrapping her arms around Agnes.

Kayla held her for several moments before pulling away. Agnes couldn't feel her touch, but the gesture still held immense meaning. Warmth flooded Agnes's chest. She felt tears begin to well in her eyes but blinked them away.

"I see you got the box of candles I stole for you," Kayla remarked gesturing to the dwindling supply on the floor. "I'll send you more when I can. I had to bribe a guard to deliver them to you. I'm sorry I couldn't smuggle you in anything to light them with. But I see the guard must have lit at least the first candle for you if you still have light," she spoke cheerfully.

Agnes's chest swelled.

'Perhaps there is still good in the universe, even in Moor…'

"Thank you, Kayla. I can't remember the last time someone showed me any kindness…" Agnes revealed.

Kayla looked at her knowingly.

"Nor I," she admitted. "But perhaps you can make it up to me when you eventually get out of here," she winked.

"It's a deal," Agnes chuckled.

A piercing scream from the neighboring cell caused the handmaidens to jolt in surprise.

"I better get out of here before the guards discover me or I'll be in here next," Kayla whispered hastily, her attention flickering to the door nervously.

"Be careful," Agnes urged her.

"I always am. Now take care of yourself and don't give up. I'll see you on the outside," Kayla promised with a sly smile and drifted back out through the cell door.

Agnes released a contented sigh as she slowly returned to her bed of hay. The dark monster that weighed her down didn't feel so heavy now. The handmaiden's visit had done more for her than any candle could. A flame of hope sparked within her as she caught a glimpse of a better life.

'I am who I am, flaws and all. But perhaps I can be more. Perhaps the first step towards a better eternity is learning to open my heart a little to let others in. Perhaps a friend like Kayla could help me keep the beast at bay.'

Agnes spent hour after hour in her cell, studying the maps of Archè's palace in the sky. She had studied each level methodically, looking for any weaknesses in its defenses, or places to hide should she fall prey to trouble. She found none. Deities as old as time itself did not make mistakes. Not after having an eon to hone their craft. They did, however, grow overconfident.

Agnes knew that cockiness made people more prone to mistakes. Agnes had learned that lesson firsthand through her own failings in her mortal life. It was her arrogance that had led to her demise. Perhaps it would be that same egotism that would bring the Gods to their knees.

Late into the night, replacing candle after candle as each wilted down to its base, Agnes meticulously studied anything and everything that might give her an advantage in her mission ahead. Including information on her own Queen.

'To know your enemy is to know their weaknesses.'

Despite having to bite her lip through wound dressing changes and frequently falling prey to coughing fits, choking on smoky air, Agnes continued to push through and learn all that she could. She doubted another soul in history had ever laid their hands upon the sacred orb, and she doubted any would again. Agnes would not waste that opportunity.

'There is a better life out there for not just me, but for people like me, and I will chase it. Maybe after I have fulfilled my *end of the bargain, Nushka will allow me to bring Kayla and others like us to the Afterworld. No soul, no matter what they have done, deserves to be sentenced to this place...'*

Agnes kept researching; the orb a cool, soothing presence in her hands despite the realm's stifling heat. A reassuring weight that she would use to its full advantage.

A shake-up was coming for the Land of the Gods, Agnes could feel it deep within her bones. Grim determination and willpower kept Agnes on task, holding her focus. She would allow nothing to stop her from seizing the power she was owed, even if it meant working alongside and submitting to the narcissistic Goddess of Blood and Bone.

The Goddess of Darkness

The atmosphere in the Hall of Shadows had changed since the Goddess of Blood and Bone's uninvited visit. Lilith's shadows stirred restlessly around the train of her black, figure-hugging gown. A strange sense of apprehension and curiosity had begun to stir within the Deity's heart.

Lilith's days were usually filled with bland indifference, an eternal monotony of fulfilling a duty that was thrust upon her because of her gifting of discernment. But Nushka's recent visit and request had unsettled the Gatekeeper to the Afterworld and she could not distinguish why. A disturbing notion for an eternal being whose gifting derived from good judgement.

From the moment Lilith had peered into her sister's dark soul, she had known her intentions were insincere. Nushka had nothing to gain from another failed attempt at invoking the rule of redemption. Why she insisted upon attempting it, the Goddess of Darkness could not determine.

'Surely my sister is not stupid enough to hope that she could deceive me. For Nushka to genuinely redeem a soul is an unattainable task,' Lilith puzzled, exhaling slowly as she massaged her temples.

'To teach her subject morality or to have them seek forgiveness for their past crimes.' Lilith shook her head. *'These qualities are beyond her. You cannot teach what you do not know…'* She pursed her lips, running a hand through her long, straight, ebony tresses.

'My sister is up to something and I will find out what it is. Not only can I distinguish a person's value as Nushka believes, but I can see and read all in the hearts of my entrusted souls. Every memory, every motive, I examine in each spirit's mind like flipping through a virtual book of their lives.'

Lilith forced herself to push aside her thoughts and focus on the task at hand. Since Nushka's arrival, she had not been as productive as usual, and the Hall of Shadows was quickly filling. With a heavy sigh and a crack of her neck, the Goddess of Darkness rose from lounging across the throne.

"Back to work," she chimed.

Lilith straightened to her full height before descending the dais stairs, her heels clicking with each light step, her long, sleek midnight hair cascading behind her.

"Who was first..." Lilith mused to herself gazing across awaiting halls occupants.

In order of their arrival, judged by the vibrancy of the light projected from each spirit, Lilith discerned and delivered eternal judgements one soul at a time. If it had taken her days or weeks, she did not know. The Goddess of Darkness did not stop to rest as she continued her work, allowing her gifting to flow over each individual soul, delving out their eternal reward or punishment accordingly.

The Goddess of Darkness administered her judgment upon tens of thousands of souls, each thoughtfully considered and appraised before revealing their eternal fates. Those who she deemed beyond redemption, whose hearts were blackened, who had committed such depravities and sought no forgiveness for their crimes, she damned to The Pitts of Moor.

As her patience wore thin, she took the time to personally punish certain individuals using her own shadow power. Lilith delighted in the opportunity to use her power and give the wretched souls a small taste of things to come before banishing them to Moor. Their screams and moans for mercy sent a thrill of electricity through her. She supposed that was how Nushka felt every day; likely part of the reason her moral compass had shattered. Lilith reined herself in.

Those who spent their lives slithering like snakes, making honey out of other people's suffering, she encased in bone and added them to her ever-growing throne. To spend an eternity watching others prosper while they could not, was poetic justice in the eyes of the eternal being. Of the countless souls she judged, most were rewarded for a life well lived and were placed under the care of Chiara.

Finally, after all the work was done, the Goddess peered at her reflection in the newly-repaired hand mirror. Her porcelain skin glowed like the moon, the shadows and wrinkles beneath her eyes vanished, and her emerald eyes were vibrant once more. Even her hair had regained its shine, her skin now taut over her slim frame. The Goddess grinned in feral delight.

"Who is the most powerful of them all now, Nushka," Lilith boasted smugly to herself.

As expected, all but a few of the souls who had graced her Hall had used their final moments to wisely praise their Goddess in attempt to sway her judgement. Their praise and worship flooded through her lifeblood, rejuvenating her strength. The energy generated through their worship wiped away signs of the Goddess's ageing and restored her power to its former glory.

After what seemed like an unending amount of work, the Goddess gratefully sat down and draped her slender legs luxuriously over the arm of the throne. The newly soul infused bones emanated a soft glow. Her shadows and power hummed gleefully around her. For no other reason than because she could, she waved her hand, transforming her slim midnight dress into a billowing gown of the deepest blue, thousands of diamonds adorning the fitted bodice. A gown fit for the Queen she was.

The whine of new souls entrapped in the throne rang in her ears. Some still begged for clemency and implored her to have their eternal fates changed. As they did so, despite the annoyance of their whines, the Goddess felt her strength continue to grow.

"Hush," she counselled the souls, wrapping her shadows around each of the glowing bones, smothering out their light. "There is no escaping this. You have all made your choices in life and now you must face the consequences..."

Soon enough they would learn to accept their fates, the fight would snuff out of them and the noise would quieten. Then peace would be once more restored to the Hall of Shadows and Lilith could finally rest.

Lilith allowed her eyes to flutter closed, her head now resting against a silk pillow she had magicked up from some hidden antechamber in the realm. The shadows trailing off her dark hair and gown leisurely uncoiled, as she allowed herself time to relax and prepare for whatever trouble Nushka's impending visit would bring.

More souls would progressively appear into the Hall of Shadows as the Goddess paused her work, that would always be the case. But they could await their eternal judgement a little longer, they had time without end ahead of them after all.

Agnes

Startled, the handmaiden woke to the sound of a guard unlocking the cell door, the keys thudding against the bone lock. The room would have been in complete darkness were it not for the ghoul guard who carried a torch in his other hand as he pushed open the cell door and stepped inside. Her forty-fifth pillar candle had long burned out. The handmaiden cringed at the reek of the ghoul's breath, smelled from her straw bed on the opposite side of the cell.

A young peuchen guard entered after the ghoul, his towering presence an intimidating sight to behold.

"Come," the peuchen hissed telepathically.

"Where are you taking me?" Agnes questioned.

"You'lll sssee," the peuchen snickered mind-to-mind.

Releasing a pained sigh, Agnes lifted herself from the bed of straw. She bit down on her lip as her blistered and burnt feet touched the scorching stone floor.

"Where are you taking me?" Agnes stammered.

"Your presssence is demanded by the missstress," the peuchen guard hissed telepathically into Agnes's mind. "Now get movvving."

Agnes gulped.

"Afffter you," the peuchen guard hissed with a twitch of his tail, gesturing for her to follow the ghoul.

Agnes hobbled defiantly after the foul-smelling phantom, biting down harder on her lip with each agonizing step. She was a warrior and had endured far worse. She would not allow a few burns to be her undoing.

With a warrior's heart, Agnes possessed a will of steel from enduring years of bullying, seen as unworthy of her title as Princess of Alearia. She had taken great pleasure in proving her siblings and the Kingdom wrong in her final years once her second, more potent gifting had awakened. Even without her mind conqueror gifting, she was still capable of so much more than people expected of her.

Agnes spent long years training as a human, honing her body into a weapon. Her mind was another, sharp as a blade and cunning as a fox. People had always made the mistake of underestimating her and she prayed the Gods were just as clueless when it came time to carry out her mission.

After all she had endured, Agnes wouldn't let a few burns and blisters bring her down. They would only serve to stoke the fire of vengeance stirring in her very being. She was a warrior, and she would not be broken.

Chin held high, Agnes slowly followed the ghoul through the dungeon corridors and up one of the bone staircases. The peuchen slithered closely behind, the talons on the ends of its tucked-in wings scraping along the bone walls as it progressed.

Rather than continuing up the levels to the throne room as she had expected, they turned down a familiar corridor and Agnes's stomach dropped. Instead of being taken before the Goddess, the wendigast leader, Hyacinth, stood over her, accompanied by several of her own wendigast handmaidens. Sinister grins spread across their faces. Their cobweb hair floated in the air escaping a fissure in the ground. The hot springs brought back a flood of mixed emotions.

Hyacinth resembled a tree spirit with her gaunt figure, long gangly limbs, tall stature, and bark-plated gown. Her handmaidens were dressed similarly, as was custom for their clan. The wendigast were a powerful race blessed with elemental magic. Over time they had learned to adapt to the mortal realms environment and utilized the herbs and natural ingredients to enhance their powers. They were the first witches to grace the mortal realm, Agnes had gleaned from the orb.

"Welcome slave," Hyacinth sneered as she gazed upon Agnes with contempt holding herself with preternatural stillness.

The High Witch's vibrant green eyes penetrated deep into Agnes's soul, as if weighing her value. Her stomach in knots, Agnes bowed before the leader of the wendigast, keeping her mouth shut, unsure of how to respond.

Hyacinth smirked at her show of reverence.

"A well-trained dog, I see," Hyacinth derided. "Though how someone as pathetic as you could be the undoing of the Gods, I cannot fathom…"

Agnes straightened at her comment. Blood boiling, fists curling, she held the leash tight on the temper that threatened to break loose.

"Why am I here?" Agnes asked. "The guard said I was summoned by the Mistress. Where is Nushka?"

Hyacinth tilted her head.

"The dog speaks. So, there is some level of intelligence there after all," she smirked, ignoring Agnes's questions completely.

The High Witch's minions snickered behind her, shadows dancing upon their fangs and gaunt features, making Agnes's skin crawl. The temptation to unleash her pent-up rage grew, but Agnes bit her tongue.

"My handmaidens and I are here to prepare you for your meeting with the Goddess of Darkness, as per your master's request," Hyacinth spat. "The Dark Goddess believes you will pave the way for our invasion. You should pray she is right. Because if you fail us, I will personally request that our Queen allows me to enslave you once she has had her fill," a predatory gleam in her eyes. "One day with me, and you will wish you were wiped away from all eternity."

Agnes stared down the High Witch, letting her see the rage burning inside her, the fury simmering in her eyes.

"Get in line, witch!" Agnes snapped, baring her teeth. "You are not the first to despise me for no reason and you will not be the last. But mark my words, when I complete my task and I am given my just rewards, I will make *you* pay for your insolence."

Hyacinth, ire in her gaze, struck Agnes across the face with her branch-like hand. The force reverberated through her jaw.

"Speak to me with such disrespect again, *slave,* and you will not exist long enough to carry out the Goddess's plan. There are plenty more desperate souls willing to carry out the Queen's bidding. Do not make the mistake of thinking yourself special!" Hyacinth seethed, emerald eyes flaring.

The leader of the wendigast turned to her handmaidens.

"You know what to do," Hyacinth ordered before she turned and stalked out of the chamber, leaving Agnes alone with five unforgiving witch spirits.

'Oh fuck.'

The wendigast witches delighted in thrashing Agnes to a pulp with their elemental magic. Though Agnes was sure the warrior race was more than capable of delving out their punishments the old-fashioned way, it appeared the handmaidens preferred to keep their hands clean. Vines summoned from another realm had pegged Agnes against the hot, hard ground, while the witches traded between funnels of boiling water and whips of wind to carry out their ministrations.

Eyes swollen shut, the fight taken out of her, Agnes lay curled up in a pitiful heap upon the rocks surrounding the hot springs. Devoid of any energy and overwhelmed with pain, Agnes could not summon so much as a snarl to her lips.

The witches had carried out their orders well. Agnes could not remember the last time she had endured such a beating, and she prayed it would be a long time before it happened again. The rocks beneath her did not scorch her skin as the dungeon floor had. Though the heat was still intolerable, giving her superficial burns from the prolonged exposure, adding to her numerous injuries.

Agnes couldn't lift her head, the pain in her corporal form insufferable. Without warning, one of the wendigast handmaidens lashed at Agnes with a wall of wind. Water enveloped her as she landed in the hot springs with a splash. Water sloshing over pool's edge from the impact, sizzled into steam. Shock overcame her as she struggled to stand to keep her head above water. Agnes hissed as her broken skin stung. Her blood dispersed into the pool around her.

"Did you enjoy our little gift?" one of the handmaidens cackled, teeth gleaming. "We are meant to heal you, to make you presentable for the Goddess of Darkness, but we could not allow such disrespect of our High Witch to go unpunished. A lesson of sorts, of what is to come if you fail at your future task. A reminder that you are nothing."

The break in the torture was a welcome reprieve.

"One day you will pay for this," Agnes vowed. She could barely make out her enemy.

"We shall see..." a sinister voice whispered in her ear, like an echo of the witch's power.

Her fellow clan members cackled in response, voicing their own creative taunts. A mouse trapped amongst a group of insatiable vultures.

The water enveloped Agnes tighter, the liquid squeezing her lungs and limbs as the witches forced the hot water to bind her like manacles. Had she been human, Agnes would have departed this realm long ago. In her current existence, even as a deceased soul in corporal form, it would take a lot more to be wiped from all eternity.

The wendigast handmaidens joined their prey in the pool. Ripples lapped at Agnes's mouth as the witches surrounded her. They towered over her with branch-like limbs, leering at her. Their wet cobweb hair clung to their scalps and necks.

"Swear that you will not speak of this to anyone, *especially* the Goddess. If you do, we'll make you wish you never crossed us. Deny our terms and we will leave you to wallow in pain until you come to your senses. Either way, we will get what we want. Do we have an accord, dog?" the wendigast handmaiden asked coolly.

Agnes's heart thundered inside her chest, her lungs begged for release. "I agree," she croaked.

Agnes could taste the wendigast handmaidens' satisfaction as they scoffed, relishing in their transgressions. Their taunts fed her ever-growing anger. She mentally added the wendigast handmaidens to the list of beings she would exact revenge upon.

Excruciatingly slowly, the witches healed Agnes's body. First the blisters, burns and cracks of open skin under her feet, then the cuts and burns to her fingers. They left the injuries they had inflicted until last, relishing in her drawn-out agony.

One by one, using their powers and herbal tinctures, the wendigast healed every cut, bruise and wound they had inflicted. The swelling and bruising around her eyes dissipated until her vision was once again clear.

Agnes peered into the water's reflection. Her eyes widened. All evidence of her injuries had been wiped away. Her skin was now perfectly pristine, her hair once more vibrant, even her eyes gleamed. The past few hours, days, had been erased from her appearance.

With her body now fully healed, the wendigast loosened their water bindings, allowing her enough range of movement to climb out of the pool. Within moments, the heat of the room had dried her. A pair of leather sandals awaited Agnes at the edge of the pool, presumably to protect her newly healed feet from the harsh environment of Moor. A gift that certainly would have come in handy days ago.

Agnes was roughly dressed in a long sleeved, full length gown that resembled something a priestess would typically wear back in her homeland. A pious dress fit for a soul seeking forgiveness for her past crimes. The wendigast arranged her hair in a tight bun. She was the picture of a woman who has seen the error of her ways and was looking for redemption. The perfect ensemble to set the scene for the ruse she was about to attempt.

D13C

The Goddess of Blood and Bone

The great hall was full to the brim of Nushka's favored souls and allies. The night's festivities were a cacophony of music, dancing and intimate encounters. It had been an age since the Goddess could recall hosting so many in her home. She ground her teeth at the overcrowded conditions.

Anticipation of the impending coup was stirring, and many of her depraved creations were behaving as if the war was already won. The hall floor was slick with wine and all manner of bodily fluids. Her guests, particularly her allied leaders, were on high alert, ready to attack at a moment's notice. Even the Dark Goddess struggled to rein in her bloodlust. Only the ever-flowing wine and their carnal urges managed to temporarily abate their cravings for violence.

Along the volcanic plains and trailing up into the jagged peaks surrounding The Pitts, ground and aerial legions of every kind were preparing for battle. Earlier, Nushka had spent time watching the peuchen legions fly in formation, their forms illuminated by the rilles in the ground radiating light. The peuchens' stealth, despite their size, was a marvel to watch.

Stretched out across the wrinkle ridges, the ghouls gathered in their hundreds. Herds of chimera with fierce heads of snake, dragon and lion, practiced drills on the volcanic plains, their paws protected from the heat by the Goddess's power.

Zeri, adopting chimera form, had joined in with the drills, perpetually floating just above the surface even as they fought, taking the opportunity to develop their fighting skills. Whether Agnes was successful or not, there would be a battle. Nushka's allies would need to unite as one army to defeat the Gods. The Deities would not go down quietly, even if rendered powerless.

In the Hall of Bone, beneath Nushka's skirts and concealed with shadow magic, a handmaiden tended to the Queen's needs. Even amongst the festivities, the Goddess still thirsted for life, still craved touch. The handmaiden wasn't particularly skilled, but her services were adequate enough.

The Goddess of Blood and Bone didn't give a second thought to the thousands gathered at the foot of her dais. Many were likewise engaged in some form or another of fornication.

A door slamming shut drew Nushka's attention. The Goddess watched on as Agnes was manhandled into the room under wendigast and peuchen guard and flung at the foot of the dais. Nushka eyes widened as she beamed at their use of force.

The handmaiden looked radiant; a far cry from the mess she would have been earlier that day. Nushka had to admit, she was impressed by the witches' healing skills.

"Leave me," Nushka commanded as she kicked the handmaiden out from beneath her skirts. The handmaiden hastily retreated out into the open and disappeared from the dais into the crowd.

"Useless whore," the Goddess cursed under her breath, incensed that her urges had not been sated. Her long ebony hair flicked in irritation at being denied.

"Sorry to interrupt you, My Queen," Agnes obnoxiously smirked at the other handmaiden's exit, drawing Nushka from her thoughts.

Like a whip, Nushka lashed one of her shadows at the handmaiden's left arm. Agnes hissed in pain as her power found its mark ripping the handmaiden's gown and leaving a nasty welt in its wake.

"My apologies for my insolence," Agnes rasped, wincing in pain as she drew her injured arm protectively up to her chest with her free hand.

Nushka sighed heavily. With a wave of her hand the gown and Agnes's arm were repaired. The Goddess took her time appraising the rest of the handmaiden from head to toe, her lip curling into a devious grin.

"As I was going to say, before you apparently needed a reminder of who holds your leash," the Queen added. Agnes flinched at her words. "It appears your leave of absence has done you well. You're practically glowing," she remarked tauntingly.

Nushka had a good feeling she knew exactly why the handmaiden's skin was so blemish free.

The Dark Goddess momentarily turned her attention to the wendigast handmaiden standing smugly at Agnes's side. She did not know her name, nor did she care. All handmaidens were useful for was serving the needs of their masters and carrying out their unwanted tasks. She only bothered to learn their names if they drew her curiosity.

Nushka was sure the wendigast's demeanor and Agnes's presentation meant that more healing than anticipated had been required. Nushka smirked knowingly. She found herself wishing that she had been present to witness the thrashing that the wendigast had likely administered. She would have reveled in seeing the handmaiden thoroughly put in her place. The Deity ruled over her minions with fear as the predominant motivator. Any extra terror installed in Agnes would only help her cause and serve as a warning of the potential consequences if she should fail in the task ahead.

"Thank you for your assistance," Nushka addressed the wendigast handmaidens with a knowing smirk. "You may now return to your High Witch."

The wendigast handmaidens bowed before the Goddess before taking their leave, their plated bark gowns dragging on the slate floor behind them.

As the hall cheered and the celebrations continued, Nushka turned her attention back to Agnes. Chocolate brown eyes met her own piecing gaze.

"Come," Nushka summoned Agnes, beckoning her with a clawed, curling finger. "It is time to re-write our fates."

Agnes

The Hall of Shadows blurred around them as hand-in-hand Nushka spirited them away. Darkness thrashed at Agnes from all angles. The kiss of darkness felt like sharp blades slashing her skin though it left no mark. The Goddess of Blood and Bone's hateful essence seemed to wrap around her, pounding at her sides, threatening to tear her apart.

Then, as quickly as it began, the shadows dissipated and that unbearable pain eased. Agnes braced her hands on her knees, panting as she tried to reel herself back together.

"What the fuck was that?!" Agnes hissed under her breath.

Nushka ignored her.

Agnes sighed; she didn't know why she had wasted her time even asking. Then she noticed the air... the temperature. Pleasantly surprised, she straightened. No longer did it feel as if her lungs were perpetually on fire. The smoke, the haze, were gone. The temperature, to her wonder, was mild. If it were not for the long sleeves of the absurd gown, she might have even needed a light coat.

'The air… Glorious fresh air… Thank the Gods for that.'

It then finally dawned upon her where she was. Like re-living a nightmare, Agnes found herself in the place her fate had been sealed five years ago. Standing before a Goddess who knew only honesty and integrity.

Her courage failed her. Agnes fell to her knees, bowing respectfully for the mighty Goddess of Darkness as she descended the dais on a cloud of floating shadows. A thin veil of mist shrouded the slate floor and now played around the handmaiden's legs, tickling her skin wherever it made contact.

The handmaiden schooled her features, transforming her face into the picture of humility. A reformed soul, she reminded herself, was who she was meant to be. Her entire existence relied on her performance in these next few moments. If she failed in her task, she may as well hand over the weapons of torture herself to the Goddess of Blood and Bone.

Agnes had heard the screaming in the dungeon, the countless souls begging for reprieve. Mercy that would never come. The term did not exist in The Pitts of Moor and it was certainly not a kindness that Nushka ever practiced.

Agnes recalled every slash, every whip and gush of water as her lungs had been filled by the wendigast handmaidens. How much torture would Nushka subject her to before finally abandoning her to the ether? It would be a kindness, to end her, rather than subject her to eternal damnation.

If she failed to convince the Goddess of Darkness that she had seen the error of her ways, she would forfeit her chance to see the Land of the Gods.

Shadows writhed around the Goddess of Darkness's voluminous ball gown of darkest night, the diamonds bedecking her corset dazzling like stars. She was power personified. Her hair of darkest night swathed behind her like silk. No claws extended like her sister. Instead, Lilith masked her cunning and power behind clothes she wore like amour.

The Goddess of Darkness approached Agnes curiously, surveying her with a long sweep of her emerald gaze. Where Nushka's emerald eyes were serpentine, Lilith's green eyes were softer, more contemplative. The Goddess drank in the image of the soul before her and smiled.

"Welcome, Agnes," she said with a silken tongue, drawing out each syllable of her name, savoring the moment.

Agnes's heart raced, and she cursed herself for projecting such weakness, fully aware the Goddess could hear every thunderous betraying beat.

"Sister…" Lilith remarked, acknowledging Nushka's existence, but barely paying her any heed.

Nushka bristled at the dismissal, but remained beside Agnes, her shadows writhing frantically. She clearly hated every moment of submission before her sister, but she held her tongue. The only time Agnes had ever seen her do so. Nushka had finally met her match.

"Greetings, sister," Nushka responded in a patronizing tone.

Holy rutting Gods. How powerful Lilith must be to disrespect her sister as such and get away with it.'

Lilith chuckled wickedly as if reading every thought in her mind.

"Oh, I most certainly am," Lilith grinned.

Agnes blanched. *Fuck.'* She froze, the realization of what that entailed hitting her like a tidal wave.

"Indeed..." Lilith purred. "Don't worry, Nushka wasn't aware until now of my range of skills either. Mind reading is simply another side effect of my discernment gifting. It has its uses, especially when vultures dare to enter my domain and attempt to deceive me."

Beside her, Nushka's eyes widened slightly, the only sign of surprise she would let show. After all, Agnes was merely a pawn to her, a toy to discard if she failed. In fact, Nushka would likely delight in her failure, as much as it would ruin her plans. But the chance to torture her favorite plaything, a way to work out her building frustration, was like dangling candy before the Deity.

"Oh, my dear sweet sister will not be torturing you," Lilith interrupted her thoughts. "At least not yet..." Lilith spoke with liquid warmth, reveling in the upper-hand she had over both Nushka and the soul before her.

Nushka launched forward, grabbing her sister aggressively by the arm, forgetting herself for a moment. Claws extended, she drew blood. Ever so slowly, Lilith tilted her head towards her sister. A beast sizing up her prey. She did not spare a glance at the wounds that had already begun clotting thanks to her immortal power, her eyes penetrating into Nushka's.

"Unhand me, before I lose my patience," Lilith counseled with deadly calm.

Rigidly, Nushka did just that, but she did not back away.

"Do not forget, Lilith," Nushka hissed, her top lip curling back to reveal her jagged teeth, "that you are not the only powerful Deity in this realm. Do not toy with me like one of your subjects."

Nushka's hair raged behind her like a wall of serpents readying to strike, her shadows gathering ominously.

"Do not threaten me in my own domain, sister," Lilith spat before turning on her heels and stalking back up the dais.

Even seething, the Divinity seated herself with liquid grace upon the throne of bone. Near identical, Agnes realized, to those in the Goddess of Blood and Bone's castle. Only larger, unfinished.

Nushka did not respond, though Agnes could see her quaking with rage. She backed away a step, wanting to place as much distance as she could between herself and the two immortals. Trying desperately to not draw attention to herself.

Lilith closed her eyes for a moment, drawing a deep breath to calm herself. Such a human mannerism, though Agnes realized the first humans were birthed by the Gods. It was more likely they had inherited the relaxation technique from their creators.

The Goddess of Darkness opened her eyes moments later, the ire in them banked to a faint glow. Her shadows seemed to have eased their frenzy, and her features calmed to a picture of grace and authority. The mask of the Goddess. An image she had honed, no doubt, over her eons of existence. The only sign of her lingering irritation was the way she tapped her fingers against her throne, a trait she and Nushka shared. Perhaps that too was a calculated action, a way of showing her growing impatience towards the Goddess who was blatantly wasting her time.

Even if Agnes spent a millennium living amongst the Gods, she did not feel it would be enough time to learn to play the game as well as they did. Yet the task ahead of her... Agnes could only hope that somehow, something miraculous could be achieved through this meeting. So far, she didn't like her chances.

Lilith turned her attention to Agnes, her steely eyed gaze penetrating deep to the core of her being, appearing to evaluate her worth.

"There is no point lying to me. I am not interested in wasting my time any further. I am interested, however, in you telling me the truth of why you think you are here. I do not care what my *sister* has promised you. If you attempt to deceive me, I will smite you where you stand and encase you in my throne of bone." The Goddess's words dripped like honey as she leaned forward. "Do you understand me?"

Agnes gulped. Her hands began quivering and she hastily clasped them behind her back. Agnes dared a quick glance at Nushka, but the Goddess only speared daggers towards her. Agnes quickly refocused her attention on Lilith, the less intimidating of the two Deities. She bit her lip and barely perceptively nodded her head.

"As you wish Goddess..." the handmaiden bowed.

The Goddess of Darkness

Like mice trapped in the claws of a mountain lion, the Goddess of Darkness had Nushka and Agnes right where she wanted them. She relished the moment, savoring the opportunity to lord her authority over her wicked sister. The ire in Nushka's gaze was truly magnificent. How she managed to contain herself... Lilith was still surprised. The scratches to her arm were nothing; the result of a child throwing a tantrum. But watching her sister finally crack and then holding power over her? That moment had been priceless.

Nushka opened her mouth to spit some spiteful retort but Lilith silenced her with a glare that had caused many souls to fall at her feet begging for forgiveness. Brow furrowed, Agnes avoided her eye contact.

The pitiful soul's presence intrigued the Dark Goddess. After all, anything was more interesting than the day-to-day cataloguing of souls and monitoring the realms. But what truly intrigued Lilith, was what she had seen within Agnes with her gifting. She wasn't sure even Agnes was aware of it. Nushka certainly had no clue.

"We had hoped to deceive you to gain passage to the Land of the Gods," Agnes confessed.

Lilith released an exasperated sigh. "Yes, that much is clear," she groaned. "But why?"

Agnes shuffled on her feet, avoiding eye contact.

"The truth is…" Agnes stammered, then pressed her lips together. Whilst fiddling with her hands, she took a steadying breath. "I thought that if I helped Nushka, that I could escape The Pitts. It would be as if I were free or as close to free as someone like me can be."

Agnes's shoulders slumped and she wrapped her arms around herself. Lilith inched forward in her chair.

"I want a better life for myself. I want to be more than I am. I want to be happy," Agnes continued. "I hate living in constant fear and in Moor, it is inescapable. Scheming and manipulating, it's all that I am good at. I'd hoped that if I could help Nushka then she would reward me with power. I thought that if I were powerful, I would finally be happy… I don't know if that's the case anymore, but it certainly couldn't make things worse," she confided.

"Interesting…" Lilith mused, leaning her chin on her hand. "You've got a long way to go to redeem yourself. Your heart is still rotten. But the seeds of change and hope, have begun to stir within and that is a curious notion indeed…" Lilith trailed off.

Agnes's eyes widened as she relaxed her arms by her side. Jaw clenched, Nushka stepped forward.

"Enough of this nonsense," Nushka lashed out.

Lilith scoffed and leaned back in her throne.

"We both know she is not redeemed so let us stop wasting time and get down to business. For too long we have been denied our rightful places amongst the Gods," Nushka pushed on. "We were sentenced to live lives that are befitting of slaves. We are capable of so much more," Nushka urged, pitching the same rubbish she had time and again.

Lilith couldn't help rolling her eyes and began cleaning her nails as Nushka droned on with the rest of her arduous speech. The aim, no doubt, to win her favor and cooperation in whatever scheme she had concocted this time.

"I have heard it all before, Nushka, and I find myself growing tired of your sacrilegious talk about revolting against our kin," Lilith reprimanded her. "What makes this plan any different?"

Nushka straightened, dark power burning in her emerald gaze.

"This time," the Goddess of Blood and Bone clarified, "I have an army ready to attack at a moment's notice. This time, we have a plan to nullify the Gods' powers. This plan will succeed," she promised. "Together, you and I will take our rightful places as Rulers of the Gods. All I need you to do is play your part. Convince Archè and Aria that this pathetic soul is redeemed, and then join me in battle. *We* will be Queens, not just of the Gods but of all realms."

"We?" Lilith narrowed her eyes.

Her shadows stilled. Lilith had heard most of it before. The offer of shared power was new, and the plan was mildly intriguing. But Lilith knew deep within there was no sincerity behind Nushka's offer.

"Yes, sister," the Goddess of Blood and Bone pushed on. "Together. We will be a team so formidable, no one will question us," Nushka declared with such fierce determination. The glimmer of hope in her sister's eyes, so strong she just *might* believe her.

A way out, that was what her sister offered. A way to end this pitiful existence as Guardian of the Gate to the Afterworld. Lilith did not think she would live to see the day Nushka shared anything. Perhaps that day had finally come.

'Maybe The Pitts has frozen over,' Lilith thought to herself.

Curiosity bloomed within Lilith as she weighed the value of her sister's words, carefully considering if the risk was worth the reward. To risk nothing would be safe, it would be comfortable. Yet Lilith had endured too many years of being *comfortable*. An existence with little to amuse, without the company of others, starved of all pleasure and manner of things that made life worth living. Her existence in the Hall of Souls, was just that—an existence. It was not the eternity she wanted for herself. It was not her destiny.

Lilith peered into Agnes's eyes, reading every thought running through her mind, weighing her value and ability to carry out the plan she saw laid out within her mind. The chance of success was slim. The Gods, especially their parents, were not stupid. They had created the mortal realms and those within them. Aria and Archè were tenacious, but they too had also grown comfortable, their rule unchallenged for far too long. They did not care about their own daughters' fates. In all her eons of guarding the Gate, not once had the Rulers checked on her or offered respite from her role. The Rulers did not care about her welfare, so Lilith reasoned it was time she stopped worrying about theirs.

Lilith took a deep breath, her heart fluttering like a hummingbird's wings. Anxiety pooled in her abdomen as her mind, gifting and heart all fought a fierce battle within her, until she finally came to a decision.

"Let's make the Gods pay," Lilith declared, allowing her shadows the freedom to roam, their eagerness for battle like an echo of her own heart. "And once we take down Aria and Archè, we can finally *live*. No longer will I be cast aside. No longer will I be banished to this realm, charged with judging the dead. The Gods have forgotten how incredibly powerful we can be, but we will remind them of our strength."

Agnes smiled hopefully. Nushka's returning grin was wild, and for a moment Lilith doubted her decision. But as quickly as the guilt surfaced, she bit down upon it and discarded it on a phantom wind. Things needed to change, and perhaps unleashing Nushka upon them was no less than what they deserved.

Guilt morphed into anger and thirst for revenge. For the first time since Lilith's sentence to the Hall of Shadows, she saw a way out. Agnes's words had resonated with her, and reminded her of the hopes she had once had for herself. The possibility of a better life dangled before her like a delectable wine.

Relishing the moment, Lilith gradually inhaled and exhaled, closing her eyes momentarily. When she opened them, her gaze met with her sister's, both her heart and mind had aligned. Her life had not been right for an awfully long time. Lilith cursed herself for enduring such an existence for so long without complaint. Apparently, all it took was a pitiful soul and an egotistical, power-hungry sibling to pull her out of her stupor.

"Let's play," Lilith declared.

Agnes released a sigh of relief at her words, but Nushka cackled with wicked amusement, and Lilith could already see all the atrocious thoughts roiling in her mind.

"I think you and I are going to make a formidable team, sister," Nushka grinned, her jagged teeth glinting in the candlelight of the Hall.

"I think so too, Nushka," Lilith smirked in return.

PART TWO

THE LAND OF THE GODS

Agnes

Sunlight.

After being trapped in the darkness for so many years, Agnes had almost forgotten there were still places where the sun shone and people thrived rather than endured. The handmaiden had long given up hope of feeling the sun's gentle rays on her face, rather than the scorching heat of the volcanic plains. Agnes had certainly never dared dream of seeing flowers bloom again, or having natural light to illuminate her path and fend off the darkness.

This place, this realm in the sky floating amongst the clouds, was the exact opposite of The Pitts. For five long years, The Pitts of Moor, where evil lurked around every corner, had been her home. A place where concepts such as safety and comfort did not exist. Here, in the Land of the Gods, anything was possible. and if their plan went well, soon it would all be theirs.

The air was crisp and fresh despite the sunny day. It had been years since Agnes had seen clouds; light and fluffy, drifting in the pale blue sky. During her mortal life, she had taken night and day for granted. In The Pitts of Moor, the only source of light was from the lava seeping out of the plains, or the many hearths and bonfires within the bone castle. The sun and moon were never visible amongst the perpetual smog. She was not even sure if they existed there at all. Agnes had spent so many years trapped in the darkness, deprived of life and light, that sensations from her human life now felt like an affront. The feeling of warmth seeping into her skin rather than scorching it surprised her.

"Welcome to The Land of the Gods," Lilith spoke gently.

Agnes was lost for words.

It had been years since Agnes had felt a gentle breeze caress her cheek and the sensation caused her to shudder. The smell of recent rain hung in the air and she inhaled deeply. The absence of pain, replaced with pleasant warmth and contentment felt surreal. Nushka's *gift* of sensation was limited in this realm, seemingly barring her destructive tendencies. So strange, the effects this unfamiliar world had on her. Even her semi-transparent spirit form seemed to glimmer in the sunlight pouring in through the castle balconies and many open windows.

The Land of the Gods: a story of myth and legend brought to life. A place of dreams and endless possibilities. Agnes recalled reading about the mythical castle in a fairy tale. She had dismissed it at the time, like so many others, as a bedtime story and nothing more. A mortal lifetime ago, back when she had been taught by the Priestesses to believe there was only one Deity, The Goddess of Darkness, who watched over all her creations—good and evil alike. Tales of Medusa, Ilbis, and other Gods were passed down from generation to generation, believed to be nothing more than folktales by humans. Stories designed to keep children from misbehaving. How naïve she had been as a human.

Agnes and many others did, however, believe the stories of the wendigast, of Hyacinth's Rise. Many reported witnessing the witch tree-spirits for themselves. Villages had offered up their family members in sacrifice to them. It still baffled her that the people had not believed in other stories too.

Hand-in-hand, the Goddess of Darkness had transported them through a portal of light and mist, directly into the receiving room of the Gods' mighty rulers; Archè and Aria. Bowing before the benevolent Rulers of the Gods, Agnes failed to control the trembling of her body.

Nushka had returned Agnes to her spirit form before Lilith had transported them to the Land of the Gods. Nushka was to wait behind until invited by the Rulers themselves. Now, it was showtime.

"The Rulers of the Gods need to be the ones to reward you by returning you to your corporal form. They will want you to be able to enjoy the festivities. Let them lap up the opportunity to demonstrate their power. It will boost their egos, if nothing else," Lilith had insisted. *"They are not aware that the ability has been passed on through the bloodline. Let us keep it that way. For all we know, I am likely capable of turning you to corporal form too since Nushka and I share so many of the same powers."*

The handmaiden remained bowed, the portrait of redemption, clad in her modest priestess gown, sunk to her knees before the dais. She waited to see how the first part of their plan would play out. If they did not overcome this first obstacle, if

Agnes and Lilith could not convince the Gods of her supposedly redeemed soul, then all their preparation would be for nothing.

The castle of the Gods was unlike anything Agnes had ever seen. More breathtaking than her wildest dreams. The multi-level castle reminded Agnes of a colosseum in a story book, floating on a bed of clouds. The building seemed completely immune to the elements, likely from whatever gifts the Gods possessed. Fountains bubbled around the room, their waters falling through the clouds and voids in the floors to the levels below like a gentle, trickling rain.

A phoenix with red and gold shining feathers and a magnificently long tail flew by the throne room's balcony, leaving a fiery trail behind it. Its entrancing yellow eyes shone bright as it briefly made eye contact with the handmaiden before continuing its path. Agnes could not believe her eyes; the phoenix was yet another story brought to life. She didn't know why she was so surprised. It seemed all the stories, myths and legends were true.

Agnes recalled a bedtime story that her mother Amealiana had read to her as a child. The tale foretold that to glimpse a phoenix brought the witness luck and good fortune. Agnes prayed that story held true. It was then that Agnes recalled the other part of the tale; if a phoenix was close, the witness was also incapable of dishonesty.

Agnes's breathing quickened, her body started to tremble. She silently prayed that the phoenix would fly away of swift wings.

Lilith placed a reassuring hand on Agnes's back.

"Just breathe," Lilith gently reassured her. "It's all going to be fine."

Upon the dais sat the imposing Deities. Aria was the sun to Archè's night. Aria radiated light, her porcelain skin glowing from within, the image enhanced by her flowing silk gown. The Deity was slender and graceful, much in the way Lilith was. Liquid light streamed from Aria's long, honey-blonde hair. The neckline of her golden, shimmering gown skimmed her collarbones, the gown itself complimenting her subtle curves, creating a beautiful silhouette.

Archè was Aria's opposite. His figure dwarfed that of his beloved; he was all muscle and trailing shadows. Agnes mused that it was his shadow magic that Nushka and Lilith had inherited, their other sister likely taking after their mother in her giftings.

Archè's eyes were dark and menacing, his chiseled features covered in thick, dark facial hair that matched the long mane tied into a bun with a leather strap. The formfitting midnight-colored tunic did little to conceal the muscles beneath. His dark leather trousers also left extraordinarily little to the imagination. Agnes, for once, was grateful she remained in her spirit form, preventing the soft blush that would have flooded her cheeks. His gruff voice drew her from her thoughts.

"Welcome, Lilith," Archè acknowledged, brow furrowed. "Why have you left your realm and requested this meeting at such haste?"

Lilith rose from her bow and straightened her back. Elegant and poised, she was the picture of an honorable daughter, though Agnes was sure she was anything but.

"Thank you for meeting us at such short notice. I would not have left the Hall of Shadows if it were not important," Lilith began. The Goddess gestured with a flourish of her hand towards

Agnes. "Over five years ago I sentenced the soul beside me to The Pitts of Moor for crimes against her family and Kingdom. It is now my privilege to introduce you to Agnes Brandistone. She was indeed a disgraced soul from Alearia, a Princess in fact. She now stands before you, seeking forgiveness for her past crimes, having seen the error of her ways. Agnes has been transformed by none other than Nushka herself," she said serenely. "She is now worthy of re-joining her loved ones in the Afterworld."

Where Nushka was chaos, Lilith was reserved, able to navigate around politics to achieve her means. Agnes watched on as the Goddess of Darkness measured every word she spoke.

Aria's turquoise eyes lit with fascination.

"Is that so, Lilith?" The Queen of the Gods said curiously, her voice light and airy, like a bird's song.

Lilith bowed her head in acknowledgement and respect for her Queen and mother.

"I was hesitant at first to believe it, My Queen," Lilith confessed. "If it were not for my unique gift of discernment, I would not have seen the truth within her declarations. Her soul has truly been rehabilitated."

Each lie fell off her tongue with such conviction that even Agnes would have believed her if she didn't know better. Archè, however, looked less than impressed by his daughter's announcement, though he seemed placated to some degree.

"I suppose Nushka redeeming a single soul was bound to happen eventually, *if* this is true. Miracles do happen," Archè remarked ironically to his wife.

Aria scorned her husband, giving him a stern glance. She was clearly much more eager to see the good in people than the King. Agnes wasn't surprised; her own parents had been the same.

"I am curious, however," the King of the Gods continued, "to hear how this miracle came to pass. Enlighten me…"

The Goddess of Darkness motioned for Agnes to stand and address the Gods, giving her a warning look the Rulers couldn't see from their positions.

Agnes curtsied before straightening to address the Rulers. Thankfully, the phoenix was no longer anywhere in sight. She released a small sigh of relief. Agnes shoulders hunched forward; her trembling was not feigned. Agnes did not make direct eye contact with the Gods, for to do so would be imprudent.

"Your Majesties," Agnes began, her voice quivering. "I am unworthy of your presence. You honor me by allowing me to stand before you."

The sudden furrowing of Archè's brow made it clear that Agnes was overcompensating, so she reined herself in, striving to find the balance between remorseful and pitiful.

"Carry on," Aria gently urged her after noticing Agnes's prolonged pause.

The Queen's sincere smile was only one of a handful Agnes had witnessed since passing into the Afterlife. Agnes offered the Queen a small, thankful smile in return. A mix of truth and lie, she realized, would be needed here.

"During my mortal life," Agnes began softly, "I did things I am not proud of. I allowed myself to be lured by the dark, powerful side of my mind conqueror gifting. I was foolish enough to think of myself as a God, rather than a mortal blessed by the

Gods. I took your gift and turned it into a weapon. I betrayed my family and my Kingdom, and for that I will never forgive myself."

Agnes pretended to take a deep, centering breath.

"For too long," she continued, sounding as earnest as she could, "we humans have forgotten our place. We have forgotten to show thanks for the blessings and giftings bestowed upon us. It is thanks to the Goddess of Blood and Bone that I was able to see the error of my wicked ways and begin to follow the path towards seeking redemption for my former life."

The thought of thanking Nushka for anything repulsed Agnes to her very core. But alas, if she did not convince the Rulers of Nushka's role in her supposed redemption, they would not allow her safe passage from Moor and her plan would be ruined.

"I know that I have wronged those who loved me," Agnes pushed on, "and I am deeply sorry for that. I want to make amends with my family. I want to rejoin them in the Afterworld, so that I can spend eternity earning their forgiveness."

Guilt twisted Agnes's stomach.

'Was that the truth?' Agnes vacillated between feelings of confusion and regret. 'Revenge doesn't hold the same allure it used to and I don't want to be alone for all eternity... Regardless, my family never cared for me anyway and they would never forgive me for what I have done.'

Archè raised a brow, wholly unconvinced, though from Aria's warm expression, she had lapped up every word like a vintage wine. Agnes didn't think the words could have sounded any more heart-felt, even if she imagined them coming from the lips of her pathetically kind-hearted sister Anastasia.

"And how exactly did the Goddess of Blood and Bone help bring about this astonishing change of heart?" Archè leered as he lounged in his throne, looking down on Agnes like an ant beneath his boot.

Agnes dropped her eyes to the ground and bit her lip, willing herself to appear virtuous.

"The Goddess of Blood and Bone employed me into her services and taught me the value of hard work," Agnes responded creatively, letting them see a glimmer of her true self. Mixing lie with truth.

"She punished me for my past crimes as was just," Agnes continued softly, "and she reminded me of my ill worth. But after I was stripped down to my very core, she slowly built me back up again. The Goddess reminded me that, despite wasting my mortal life on spiteful revenge, my former choices did not have to impact my eternity.

"It was through her actions that I realized I could strive to be worthy of my family and of the Afterworld, if only I sought forgiveness and cut away vengeful thoughts that had consumed my past life. She taught me how to forgive myself, so that I could move on and become a better version of myself. The strings holding me back in the past have been severed, and standing before you is a soul who knows she is unworthy, but seeks to be more," Agnes confessed, the lies and truth seamlessly intertwined.

Agnes straightened her back. "If I am granted safe passage to the Land of Milk and Honey, I will first seek forgiveness from my family. If they choose to accept me, and it will be their choice, then together we will spend eternity making up for all the time we lost whilst I was consumed by hate and rage," Agnes promised sincerely, surprising even herself.

Aria seemed impressed, and even Archè seemed to weigh her words with more value. Lilith, who remained by Agnes's side, relaxed her shoulders a little too, as if she had also felt the shift in the room. Perhaps Lilith had even noticed a change in the King's thoughts, thanks to her gifting.

Archè made eye contact with his wife, the two seeming to debate their decision telepathically between themselves. Agnes waited anxiously for them to deliver their decision, her fate hanging precariously in the balance.

After several long minutes that felt like a lifetime to Agnes, The King of the Gods turned to Lilith and made his request. "Summon Nushka to our domain. It seems we have cause for celebration." Sitting beside him, the Queen of the Gods beamed in delight.

Agnes brought a hand to her gaping mouth. The handmaiden tried to not get her hopes up. She would believe their sincerity when Nushka was in the Land of the Gods with them. Even then, she knew she would be looking over her shoulder every second, waiting for the Rulers to change their minds and send her back to Moor.

"Welcome to your new life, Agnes," Aria trilled warmly. "The Afterworld awaits you, but first we must celebrate with your mentor, Nushka. You will be both be our guests of honor at tonight's ball."

With a flourish of her hand and a flash of blinding light, Agnes transformed from her spirit form into corporal form. A gown of glimmering silver fabric that felt as light and soft as a cloud now draped elegantly across her frame. Agnes couldn't help the surprise that filled her eyes as she offered the Queen of the Gods a quizzical look.

"Consider the physical form and the gown a gift," Aria offered sincerely. "A rare reward for all you have overcome to stand before us today. Use these gifts for whatever pleasure you wish to engage in during your stay, and when the time comes for Chiara to welcome you into the Afterworld, you will be returned to your spirit form, forever free of pain, ageless and beautiful." The Goddess smiled.

"Thank you, Your Majesty," Agnes bowed low, holding back the grin that threatened to spread across her lips.

'Just like that, the lamb has welcomed the lion into her lair.'

Aria and Archè descended their thrones and exited, leaving only the Goddess of Darkness and Agnes behind. A triumphant smile spread across Agnes's face, a feeling of accomplishment welling within, but her mission was not over. She had only passed her first task. The next stage in their plan bordered on impossible.

The Goddess of Darkness appraised Agnes with smug satisfaction. "Well played, Agnes. Perhaps one day you might have legitimately earned your place in the Afterworld after all... I didn't think such a think were possible. Regardless, our plan remains the same. I will become a Ruler of the Gods. Do not fail in your next task. If you do, the fate awaiting you is something I would not wish upon my worst enemy."

In a barely perceptible movement, Lilith removed a vial filled with transparent liquid from her pocket and tucked it discretely into the hidden side pocket of Agnes's gown.

"Do not disappoint us," Lilith warned before disappearing through a portal of light and mist, leaving Agnes utterly alone in a strange new realm.

Agnes

The suite was more opulent than anywhere Agnes had ever stayed, including her Royal suite in Alearia. The room was airy, with large, open windows. With the Gods commanding the weather, there would never be a need to close them.

Shortly after the Goddess of Darkness had left her alone in the receiving room, a servant had escorted her to a guest suite to await the evening's festivities. Agnes thought it absurd that a minor Deity fulfilled the role of a servant, much less waiting on a soul from The Pitts.

Tonight, the Rulers of the Gods would be hosting a ball in her honor. An elaborate gathering to honor a wretched soul from Moor and a narcissistic Goddess; the Deities had lost their minds. The Queen of the Gods would likely throw a celebration in honor of a newborn pegasus; the idea of it was completely irrational. Of course, Nushka and Agnes had predicted this would happen. The upcoming ball was an essential part of the next phase of their plan. Without the cause for revelry, their plan would be doomed. But the more Agnes thought about the entire situation, the more illogical it seemed.

The running bath in the adjoining bathing chamber bubbled away. The scent of lavender oil immersed in water floated towards her on a gentle breeze. The bath was another wasteful display of the Gods' good fortune. Agnes had no need to bathe, nor did she want their pity offering. After the wendigast had finished *punishing* her for her insolence, they had healed and polished her skin in the hot springs until she was gleaming. It would likely be a while until Agnes would feel comfortable soaking in warm water again. She couldn't believe that had only been last night. After several slow and agonizing days in the bone castle's dungeon, the past day had flown by in a blur.

Agnes shook her head in disbelief. *'Why would Lilith suggest I could ever fully redeem myself? The idea is absurd. I still want to claim my seat or power. My goals have not changed. I will do whatever it takes to attain it. That doesn't seem like a very virtuous thing to me… It might not bring me happiness. There is no guarantee. But at least I will finally be a Queen of a realm. I will finally have earned the power that I have always been denied in both this life and in Alearia.'* She ran a hand through her blond tresses, closing her eyes for a moment.

"I need to focus," she coached herself.

Agnes strolled to the open balcony of her suite, eager to get a better sense of her surroundings, recalling the castle's blueprints she had gleaned from the Orb. The truth-inspiring phoenix with its fiery tail feathers had returned to circle around the uppermost parapets of the castle.

Below her, the floating building descended through the clouds, past her level of sight. Layers upon layers of wispy clouds wound throughout the open buildings, the occasional waterfall descending from one balcony to the next from extravagant water features.

Agnes had no idea how the Land of the Gods existed. Its very creation defied gravity and all logic. How the structures remained perpetually suspended in the sky was a mystery that Agnes had been unable to discover in her research. Without visual evidence of land below, Agnes questioned if the city in the sky acted like its own planet, defying all rules that the mortal realms were bound to. She supposed it wasn't a huge stretch of the imagination, given the Gods were literally the creators of all existence. Creating a whole realm that existed beyond anything else seemed like just the kind of extravagant thing the Gods would do.

'Perhaps this realm was the birthplace of all others,' Agnes mused. 'If only I had more time to scroll through the Orb, to learn everything I could about the Gods and their history. There wouldn't be enough time to glean all the information stored within the relic.'

Drawing herself away from the awe-inspiring view and her musings, Agnes forced herself to focus on the mission. She had only hours to contaminate the Gods' drinking supply before the ball began. From the castle maps she had studied within the Orb, she knew she was currently several levels above the main entertaining areas of the castle. The kitchens were a level below those again. The running bath and out-of-reach waterfalls were the only signs of water sources from her suite. Agnes was left with only two choices. Her first option was to sneak down to the kitchens, where she might find the cellars and taint the wine. Her second option was to try and locate the castle's water supply and taint it with the magical tonic. The first option, she gambled, was more likely to succeed.

Making her way to the main suite door, Agnes was surprised to note the door had been left unlocked. A sign of *trust*. The thought of anyone trusting her caused an unfamiliar feeling to suddenly weigh her down; something she had not felt for a long time... until today. Shaking off the useless feeling of guilt, she reminded herself of the power and reward that would come her way if she did not fail her task. Refocused, Agnes pushed down on the door handle, pulling it open towards her to reveal a shirtless warrior slouching against the hallway wall. He was dressed in very tight leather pants and glaring right at her.

"Going somewhere?" the younger version of the King of Gods questioned. His thick, gruff accent, laced with contempt, reminded her of the legionaries from Stanthorpe, a neighboring Kingdom of Alearia. An accent that usually featured a soft burr emphasizing the letter 'r' as they spoke. The warrior's brown glowering eyes stared straight through her.

Agnes sighed exasperatedly.

The male pushed off the wall and strode towards her, forcing Agnes to withdraw back into her suite. As soon as the Deity was inside, he slammed the door shut behind him. His intensity had even Agnes, with her heart of steel, caught off guard. Before she had a chance to dodge out of the way, he grabbed her by the arm with an unbreakable grip, a sinister grin promising pain now in place. Whoever this warrior was, he had to be highly ranked to have been made aware of her arrival only minutes after she had left the receiving room. Unlike the Queen of the Gods, this brute had no intention of welcoming her with open arms.

Surprise must have flashed across her face because his predatory grin grew even more menacing. Agnes ground her teeth. This shit had the King of the Gods written all over it.

"Unhand me you son-of-a-centaur!" Agnes seethed, trying to pull her arm free from his grip.

She internally cursed her weak muscles, that were unable to fend him off, but thankfully she no longer felt pain. In her former body, trained as a warrior, she would have stood a good chance of outmaneuvering him.

"Or what?" the stranger demanded. "You'll go to the Rulers and complain about me? *Who* do you think sent me?"

Agnes saw red, trying with all her might to pull out of his grasp. She risked tearing her eyes away from the intruder, having nothing to lose, setting her sights on anything that could potentially be used as a weapon to defend herself. Other than the bedding and linen, everything else was secured to the ground or wall *as if...* as if this were an ornately styled prison. A place to accommodate beings the Rulers did not wholly trust but wanted to appear amicable towards.

Agnes pushed back into the male, a futile attempt to get him off balance, recalling her hand-to-hand combat training. But he was ready for her, his stance grounded, having the foresight and experience to anticipate such a move.

"As if such a move could outmaneuver the God of War," he ridiculed.

Before Agnes had time to react or defend herself, the immortal swept a leg forcefully beneath her. She hit the ground an instant before he pounced atop her. Quicker than Agnes could register, the God of War pegged her arms above her head with one hand. Then he immobilized her legs with his knees, preventing her from kneeing him in any particularly sensitive areas. Agnes awaited the usual jolt of pain that would come from such a lashing, but it didn't come. In that moment, Agnes couldn't have been more grateful for whatever magic this realm possessed that nullified her gift from the Goddess of Blood and Bone.

"Holy fucking Gods," Agnes breathed.

Thorn, the God of War, in all his half-naked perfection, had her pinned to the ground, towering over her. Agnes couldn't help but look towards the dip of his abdominal muscles that began descending into those gloriously tight pants of his. Had he not been so intent on harming or interrogating her, the action would have caused an ache to build between her legs.

"How do you want to play this? Shall we skip the foreplay and just get down and dirty or did you have something else in mind?" Agnes teased, trying to regain some semblance of control.

A flash of amusement glimmered in his eyes as he maintained his firm grasp on her arms.

"I'm glad to see you have shed the false pretenses and cut to the chase. It will save us so much time," he said gruffly.

"I'd rather listen to you read a romance novel. It appears you don't always get what you want," Agnes quipped. She was positive that husky accent had sent many damsels to their knees.

The God's nostrils flared, his eyes narrowed.

Agnes tried to wiggle her legs free, but the weight and position of him made it impossible. Darkness seeped from the God, trailing up her arms and down her legs before finding purchase and wrapping around her wrists and ankles like enchanted shackles. When Agnes dared test the strength of its power by pulling on her bindings, she earned herself a jolt of electricity in response, causing her to hiss in pain. Perhaps Thorn was so powerful he could override the magic of this place. She supposed he was the God of War, after all. Delving out pain was his general occupation.

"Bastard!" she cursed. "If you could have done that all along, why didn't you?! Get off me!"

"Now where would the fun be in that?" Thorn answered smoothly as he stared into her brown eyes.

A rush of warmth flooded her core. For too long she had craved being in this position with a man, and he was as hot as the damn Pitts. She internally cursed the scent she was likely projecting towards her captor, though Thorn was apparently enough of a gentleman not to draw attention to it. At least for now.

Thorn ever so slowly eased off her body before rising and taking his time to lazily stretch out on the chaise beside her, leather boots and all. The arrogant bastard even had the gall to fold his arms behind his head as if he were enjoying the entertainment, or perhaps he was relishing the effect he had on her.

'Prick, such an absolute cocky prick!'

Agnes pulled herself up, still grateful for the minor abdominal strength allowing her to do so. Such an action would have been as easy as breathing in her former life. As a warrior she had honed her body into a weapon, her mind equally as sharp. Now all that remained was a form barely able to carry out basic tasks. Another aspect of herself that that afterlife had taken from her.

Agnes deserved it all: every punishment, every misfortune. She knew that deep down in the small part of her that still felt empathy and remorse, but it didn't mean she couldn't resent every moment of it. She was determined to make the Gods pay for their role in her powerlessness. The Goddess of Blood and Bone was right about one thing, as much as it pained her to acknowledge it. For too long the Gods and Goddesses had unchecked power over the universe. For too long had they been free to control and manipulate people's lives as they saw fit. They had too much damn control over everything and only those they saw as *worthy* benefitted from their supposed benevolence. The power balance needed to be disturbed.

"Done daydreaming, Princess?" The God of War inquired, one eyebrow raised.

Even shackled, Agnes made a vulgar gesture towards him that sent the God chuckling.

"That's more like it," he said, sitting upright on the edge of the chaise.

He edged forward, his arms resting upon his bent knees as he leaned over her. Agnes took in every honed muscle of his chest and arms, and knew there was no escaping whatever Thorn had planned.

"Where were you planning to go when you tried to leave your room?" he asked intently.

Agnes glared at him, shaking her bound wrists.

"I would be much more amicable if you would unbind me! I didn't realize I was a prisoner!"

"Nice try but that's not going to happen," he stated.

Agnes rolled her eyes. "Why am I not surprised?" she muttered.

Thorn leaned closer so that his mouth hovered mere inches from her face. Agnes felt a shiver ripple down her spine at the feeling of his breath caressing her ear.

"I can see why my sister kept you around for so long," he whispered huskily. "There is fire within you. A fire that I would have very much enjoyed tasting for myself. If you were not already *used* goods."

Agnes slammed her head to the side to harm him, but Thorn was too quick. Anticipating the move, he straightened. Thorn looked down at her with that same cocky expression he had worn before. The God of War was baiting her, and she knew it.

"Now that wasn't very nice, was it?" he advised, shaking his head.

Agnes spat at his feet and the God flashed his teeth at her in disgust.

"Unbind me or I will tell the Goddess of Blood and Bone exactly how you have been mistreating her *goods*," she seethed. Revulsion burned within her at the taste of the last word on her tongue.

The God's laugh rumbled. "Do not delude yourself into thinking that my sister cares for you. She cares for no-one but herself."

'*Well, it's true,*' Agnes thought bitterly, feeling a stab of self-pity spear her heart. '*Even in the hot springs she did not care for me, only my flesh. It was desperate and stupid of me to play that card on Thorn. It was always about sex for Nushka. An agreement between us, that I tended to the Goddess's needs in return for my safety in Moor. It was meaningless to the Goddess, a carnal joining, and I was just another one of her handmaidens.*'

"I know that your master has gathered her forces," Thorn stated in a low voice, drawing Agnes from her thoughts.

Agnes stilled at the accusation, a million thoughts rushing through her mind. She had only a moment to decide how to proceed.

"I don't know what you're talking about, God."

The God of War appraised her with deep, calculating brown eyes. A sly grin formed on his face that Agnes knew meant trouble, and not the good kind.

"Whatever you are thinking, forget it," she demanded. "I don't know anything."

If only I had my freedom and former strength and I would really put this son-of-a-centaur—'

Without warning, a dark wind hauled Agnes from the ground lifting her several feet into the air, wrists and arms still bound. Agnes couldn't see more than an inch in front of her as a tempest of dark magic swirled around, lashing at her gown and bare skin. Agnes clenched her teeth as the torture ensued. The pain was horrendous, worse than everything the wendigast witches had subjected her to. Even worse than the bite that had been her death blow, ripping out her throat.

A silver dagger penetrated the dark wind and steadily traced the length of her sternum, causing a torrent of pain that had Agnes hissing through her teeth. The dagger tracked lower and lower down her body, agonizingly ripping her muscles in two. The tang of blood coated her tongue as she bit down on her lip unable to bare the pain. But she would not scream, she would not give Thorn the satisfaction. Lower and lower the dagger descended, past her navel and stopping just short of her underwear before dropping to the ground beneath her, clanging on the porcelain tiles.

The swirl of dark magic dissipated, and Agnes greedily inhaled the fresh air. Her body remained hovering just above the ground, and the evidence of what the God of War had done to her was devastating. The gown gifted to her by Aria gaped open right down to her delicates. Every inch of skin where the dagger had pierced bore a thick black scar, like nothing Agnes had ever witnessed. Not a trace of blood from any of her wounds remained, as if the dark magic had washed it away before retreating into its unholy master.

The God of War stood a foot in front of her now, all false pretenses cast away. Before Agnes stood a mighty warrior, a Deity who determined the fates of Kingdoms, the creator of swordsmanship and other weaponry skills. For the first time in Agnes's existence, she truly felt small. As insignificant as a grain of sand.

"That was a warning of things to come if you do not answer my questions honestly." Fire blazed in his eyes, a glimmer of the dark magic she had just witnessed ready to pounce at its master's command.

She gulped and nodded her head, feeling wholly outmatched.

"Smart girl," Thorn cooed before lowering her back to the ground and unbinding her from his magical restraints.

Agnes did not run or call for help. She knew both would be pointless. If Thorn wanted to harm her, she wouldn't make it to the door before he had a chance to do so. A warrior who had spent a millennium refining his craft, who had created the warfare rule books. The God of War stood forebodingly before her in all his chiseled glory.

Agnes felt her knees wobble and she stepped back until she felt the edge of the bed behind her. Legs trembling and unable to support her any longer, she took a seat.

Thorn resumed his position on the chaise opposite her, his arms relaxed on the arm of the chair. Powerful. These Gods were so incredibly old and powerful. A fact that Agnes had somehow managed to forget. Her entire lifetime would have seemed like the blink of an eye to the God of War. In that moment, she wasn't sure how Lilith or Nushka had ever had any faith in her ability to outsmart their kin. She was in so far over her head that her cockiness had gotten the better of her, and she had forgotten who her enemies were.

"As I was saying…" the God resumed, "I am aware that Nushka's creations have gathered in The Pitts of Moor. I know that because it is my duty to keep tabs on such things. She has been readying her forces for some time… and I have been watching." Thorn claimed with that husky accent.

'If he knows so much, then why hasn't he said anything to the Rulers of the Gods? They must not know, or they would have attacked The Pitts with their full Godly strength already,' Agnes mused. She tucked the piece of information away, unsure what it meant for their cause.

"If you know everything already, then what do you want from me?" Agnes asked crossing her arms.

Thorn relaxed in his chair, apparently taking Agnes's resignation to finally cooperate as a sign she wasn't about to attempt anything stupid. The God of War sent a probing wisp of dark magic over Agnes that poked and prodded at her skin, leaving goosebumps in its wake. The touch felt so incredibly close to a violation, but Agnes allowed it to continue for now, knowing that it would be reckless to risk provoking the God before her. The magic disappeared as quickly as it had arrived, much to Agnes's bewilderment.

Thorn abruptly moved to the edge of his seat. Leaning forward, lip curled; he glared at her in disgust.

"What is in the vial?" Thorn asked with deathly quiet.

When she did not immediately respond, he launched himself at her, grasping her wrist once more to shake her.

"Were you planning to kill us all with poison? Was that my sister's grand plan?!" He roared.

Agnes sat stunned, a tremor of terror vibrating through her body at the ire in his eyes.

"Not to kill," Agnes confessed, hoping the truth paid off. "Such magic does not exist to kill a God. Only to nullify their powers."

Thorn released her, taken aback for a moment.

"Fuck," he groaned, brushing a hand through his shoulder length, brunette locks.

Dark fire raged in his eyes as he strode, fists clenched across the room to pour himself a stiff drink. Agnes hadn't noticed the decanter earlier. Perhaps he had summoned it with whatever dark magic wrestled beneath his taut skin.

One shot, then another passed his lips before he lifted the crystal decanter and took a long, long swig. After drinking most of the amber liquid, he slammed it back on the cabinet top, shuddering the furniture. He leaned his hands on the cabinet as if to steady himself or process whatever it was that was going through his mind. Agnes couldn't tear her eyes away from him.

The God of War

The plan was sound. Basic and predictable, but sound. Thorn knew that arrogance would be the downfall of the Land of the Gods one day, and that day might have arrived. In the eras he had watched over the mortal realms, Thorn had utilized every tactical strategy imaginable. In the end, it was always complacency that was a Kingdom's biggest downfall. Too often did a Kingdom of immense power became blind to potential threats against them, over-confident in their defenses and abilities.

In recent times it had almost been Alearia's downfall. By Deity standards, the several mortal years since the Battle of Alearia had ended seemed like mere days ago to the God of War, and he was still hostile about the outcome. Stanthorpe, the invading Kingdom, had been one of his most prized Kingdoms. An entire territory of warriors who fought with their swords first and asked questions later. A stupid bet had meant that the Kingdom of Stanthorpe now fell under his sister Lilith's domain. The loss had meant reduced worshippers to strengthen Thorn's powers. Since he also gained power from all wars regardless of their location, the loss was not as significant as it would have been for his sister had the fates not fallen in her favor.

Thorn straightened his back and breathed deeply.

"I've seen this coming for a while," he confessed to Agnes. He didn't know why he was confiding in her since he owed her nothing. Perhaps he just needed to talk.

"The first sign something was amiss, was the decreased activity in the mortal realms," Thorn continued. "The wicked creatures' numbers had been dwindling for some time and, initially, I'd thought they might have been poached and killed into near extinction. But Nushka must have been slowly retreating them to The Pitts. I fucking knew she was raising an army!"

Thorn slammed his first on the cabinet, cracking the glass top. He ignored the choked sound that escaped the girl behind him. Thorn poured himself another knuckle of whisky and gulped it down. The amber liquid burned like The Pitts but it helped take the edge off.

"What astonishes me the most is Lilith's involvement," he confessed. "Since you're clearly only here as Nushka's pawn, there is no way in Moor that you managed to deceive her or prove your worth, she has to be involved in all this."

Agnes said nothing, just sat there and took in his words. Likely trying to glean any way to use his ramblings against him. He didn't care. No one would believe her if she tried to rat him out for keeping his theories to himself.

'Perhaps the endless, monotonous years of isolation and guarding the Gates have turned Lilith's heart sour,' Thorn mused. *'Though, I saw the way she favored her people during the war, especially the former young Queen. Lilith's heart is virtuous at its core, but perhaps the eternity she was subjected to is not enough for her.*

'Nushka had always been the type to crave power. An act of rebellion from her was inevitable. You can only keep an animal trapped for so long before it turns on you. Perhaps ruling over a domain and guarding the Gates to the Afterworld, is no longer enough for Lilith either.'

"If you knew about Nushka's gathered forces, why haven't you reported her to Archè and Aria?" Agnes asked, curiosity likely getting the better of her.

'And that's the real question, isn't it…?'

Thorn whirled around to face the maiden. He could feel the wrath simmering beneath his skin, begging for an outlet. Perhaps he would practice his training upon the handmaiden in punishment for her from aiding in all this mess.

"Do not push me, soul, I have not yet decided what to do with you. You may have earned my sisters' trust to some small degree, but you have not earned the right to question us. It would do you well to remember who and what I am. If I were you, I would be begging for mercy," Thorn warned.

Nushka's subject held up her hand defensively to placate him, muttering her insincere apologies as she did so. Thorn ignored her entirely as he took a long swig from the second bottle of aged, honeyed whiskey he had summoned, making his way to the chaise. He felt Agnes's heavy gaze monitoring his every move.

"I was sent here by Archè to interrogate you. He's suspicious of you. He doesn't care about you personally, he wants to know Nushka's true intentions and sent me to find out if it's all a sham," Thorn disclosed, not bothering to make eye contact with her.

A gentle breeze made the sheer curtains hanging from the windows flutter. A moment passed and the God turned his head curiously towards the girl who had not responded. He recognized the look painted across her face. It was the same calculating expression that graced his own when he monitored the wars between Kingdoms and weighed his next move. She was a clever fox.

Thorn rose a brow, daring her to make a smart remark. He could see how she had drawn her sister's attention. She was pretty enough for a human; he had said as much earlier. But her real appeal was her fiery spirit. He wouldn't have minded taking her for a ride and seeing what all the fuss was about. It had been a week since he'd had a good fuck.

Nushka's minion opened and closed her mouth several times, weighing her words. The God sighed exasperatedly. With his right hand, Thorn withdrew a blade from the sheath at his left hip. Without a second thought, he flung the dagger at her, the blade landing a hairs-breadth from her left leg. It embedded in the mattress with a soft thud. The action had the desired effect.

"Fucking arsehole! What did you do that for?!" Agnes hissed, withdrawing the blade from the mattress beside her and flinging it towards him.

Thorn caught the blade in his hand with little difficulty, but a flutter of surprise and delight momentarily warmed his core.

"You truly have nothing to say about my claims that the Ruler of the Gods has sent me to interrogate you?" Thorn asked.

"What is it that you want me to say? I'm not surprised in the slightest; I would do the same in his position," Agnes shrugged her shoulders, a mocking tone creeping into her voice. "The real question is why you haven't already gone crawling back to Archè to tell him about the potion or the gathered forces. Could it be that perhaps you have had enough of living in the shadows of the mighty Rulers as well?"

Surprise jostled through the God of War's veins.

'How is it that she has the gall to question me so brazenly and why is it that I'm mildly impressed by that?' Thorn mused.

"My motives are none of your concern, soul," he replied dryly, leaning back in his seat. "But while we are on the subject, how exactly where you planning to poison us all? I assume it would have been at the ball while we were all gathered. That's how I would have played it."

Agnes leaned forward, mild amusement now lining her features as she appeared convinced he wasn't in a rush to report back to his Rulers.

"Why would I tell you?" Agnes raised a brow. "Are you offering to help?" She gently pushed. An innocent enough question to gauge where his loyalties lay.

Thorn threw his head back and laughed. "Why exactly would I want to help poison myself?"

"Why would you not?" she winked.

Thorn's answering smile reached his dimples. "Okay, now I can see why you must amuse my sister so. You have no fear! Even sitting before a God as old and powerful as the ages, you still act as if your very existence is not under threat, as if I couldn't smite you where you sit."

The weight of the situation lay thickly upon Thorn's shoulders and he welcomed the banter that gave him a moments reprieve. The choice before him was unnervingly clear if he was truly honest with himself. Subconsciously, he had picked his side long before Agnes had been brought to the Land of the Gods.

Thorn knew he should have gone to Archè and Aria as soon as he noticed Nushka's followers beginning their retreat. He should have gathered his own forces to retaliate as was his role amongst the mortals and Gods. But he had done neither. Instead, he had looked the other way.

The God of War had been biding his time for a while. Lilith's act of rebellion had been the final nail in the coffin. He had always been closer to Lilith than his other siblings. Chiara, their parents' favorite, lived the life of contentment ruling over the Afterworld. The remaining three siblings had been banished to different corners of the universe. For a long time now, Thorn had pondered their sentences. It seemed all too convenient that four of the most powerful Gods and siblings would be separated from each other.

'Perhaps we weren't separated for the mortals' sakes, but for those of the Rulers. Together, my sisters and I would have been an insuperable team. Any one of us would have posed a threat to our parents' rule. So rather than see us flourish, they banished us to rule over different realms, never to have contact with each other again. Archè and Aria were so paranoid of any threat to their title, they banished their own children. Though I wasn't given a realm

to rule over, my position keeps me eternally busy. There was always a power-struggle or war to manage.

'Compared to Lilith and Nushka, my immortal life-span would have seemed like a dream, confined as they were to their desolate realms. All the while I stood by idly, never fully considering how badly they suffered, how powerless they had been rendered when, really, their giftings might have outmatched us all.'

"So why haven't you gone to Archè, Thorn?" Agnes brazenly pushed.

This time when he looked at Agnes, he saw a lot of his younger self in her. He recognized the familiar brash, wild disregard for rules. He saw her fighting spirit and the potential she had to be so much more if only she were given the chance.

He stared into Agnes's deep brown eyes and when she did not shy from his gaze, he spoke candidly. "I have been alive for a long time... I have witnessed many battles, but none as devastating as the battle that is to come. Archè and Aria's rule has never been challenged in all my years of existence."

He paused for a moment to take another swig of the amber liquid straight out of the bottle.

"My parents view Nushka as a petulant child deserving of chastising," Thorn sadly revealed, his shoulders slumped. "Even Archè, despite your part in this, will not see Nushka's betrayal coming. My father thinks she is trying to deceive him purely so she can return home and live the life of luxury like all the other spoilt Deities here. Archè won't foresee the power play she will make, and he certainly will not believe that Lilith would conspire against him. I will not sit by and allow my sisters to be mistreated any longer.

For too long have I justified their banishments as for the greater good. It is time that I stood by them once more."

The God of War waved his hand and a table appeared between them. A heartbeat later, decanters of wine began materializing atop the table, each almost full to the brim with rich red wine. The type of wine that made you forget your own name and had you reaching for comfort in the arms of a stranger. The fruity wine was unique to the Gods, so much more potent than anything created by mortals.

"Do what you came here to do and let us be done with it," Thorn said sadly, gesturing towards the crystalware atop the table.

Agnes looked at Thorn as if he had grown four horns and had sprouted warts all over his face. After a few heartbeats, she must have gauged that he wasn't setting her up to trap her, as she turned to appraise the dozens of wine jugs before her. This particular wine was reserved for occasions such as these. He knew these exact bottles would be served at the banquet that night because he had taken them directly from the kitchen cellar. It was the only option as far as Thorn was concerned for the plan to succeed.

The handmaiden looked up at the God of War again and raised a brow in question, to which he simply nodded shallowly in acknowledgement. There would be no going back after this. He had made his choice, he had picked his side. Now he could only hope that he had chosen wisely, for if Archè found out about the epic betrayal, his eternal life would be forfeit.

Agnes rose from the bed on unsteady feet, retrieving the small glass vial from her pocket. The gown he had destroyed earlier remained gaping open, and a flicker of remorse flushed through

Thorn at the sight of her. With a quick flick of his magic, the tattered material was replaced with an elegant silk ball gown of the deepest red, adorned with tiny glimmering diamonds. The gown would be revered by any of the Goddesses and would be another weapon in her arsenal. Another thought had her golden blonde hair brushed and life returned to the dull tresses. Even Thorn could admit she looked devastatingly beautiful, like a Princess without a crown. She was a deadly serpent wrapped as a pretty gift. She was ready to strike... and he was willing to help her.

'*Goddess help them all,*' he thought, smirking at the irony.

The Goddess of Blood and Bone

The summons from the Rulers had come much more promptly than the Goddess of Blood and Bone had anticipated. She would have preferred to have accompanied Agnes to her initial meeting with the Rulers of the Gods. However, once her sister had pointed out that her abrasive side may not have helped the situation, it was decided she would stay behind and leave the smooth talking to Lilith. Nushka could not fault her sister's logic, though the lack of control over the situation had exasperated her.

Lilith and Nushka now sat at the formal dining table in the Castle of the Gods; a place where they had endured many arduous court gatherings as younglings under her parents' rule. This family luncheon promised to be just as arduous as the formal family dinners she had attended as a child.

Nushka wasn't sure how her sister envisioned their future other than ruling side-by-side. Growing up, The Goddess of

180

Darkness had always been the one to follow the rules. Lilith's gift of discernment also meant that she was a walking, talking lie detector as a youngling—a fact that Nushka and Thorn, the mischievous siblings, had found particularly maddening. The idea of her joining the cause was still quite unexpected.

The décor and lighting in the room stung Nushka's eyes. All the bright white furniture, the flooding natural light and clean air was strange to the Goddess of Blood and Bone's senses. After eons spent in darkness, the bright and airy room was repulsive to her.

'This is yet another one of the many reasons they must pay,' Nushka promised herself. *'While I have been living amongst the rabble in the darkness and Lilith has been isolated from the realms, they have been living the life of luxury. For most of the Deities, their biggest concern is what to have for dinner or tracking their power levels. Utter nonsense, all of it. But that will all change when I am in charge. We will make them pay for all we have endured.'*

Beside Nushka at the table, Lilith was engaged in bland conversation with their mother about the rate of soul ascensions into the Land of Milk and Honey. Apparently, genuinely good souls were harder and harder to find these days, and so the number of ascensions to the Afterworld had dropped significantly over the last few centuries. Nushka was not in the least bit surprised given the increased number of souls delivered to her over the years. Souls she had delighted in delivering their eternal punishments to. A task that now brought her less amusement than it once had.

Nushka had appointed her first handmaiden to distract her from the eternal monotony of her role. From there, her harem had only grown. She would have no need of them once she ruled The Land of the Gods. Here, in this domain, she could have anyone she chose. Deities, male and female alike, would flock to her just to gain an inch of power. Nushka licked her lips at the thought, momentarily lost in the prospect of it all.

Nushka picked up the glass of wine before her and swirled the deep red liquid, the color reminding her of rich blood. Such reactions had become second nature to her after an eternity ruling over a realm of torture and depravity.

Neither Lilith nor Nushka planned to consume a single drop of liquid at the ball, lest they fall prey to their own scheme. In the meantime, the Goddesses relished each drop from their glasses, reveling in the potency and aphrodisiac-instilling qualities. As an extra precaution, this bottle and the bottle of wine from which Lilith drank, she had brought with her from The Pitts masked as a gift for the Ruler's. Perhaps she would find a lesser Deity to warm her bed and shake off some of her unease before the grand ball began and her plan was underway. She mused that it would be harder to find time for such luxuries once all hell had literally broken out.

"Nushka," Aria addressed her in that singsong voice her daughter could identify from a room away. "We are so happy to have you and your sister back home with us. I cannot express how proud I am of you both for all that you have achieved over the years. Ruling over The Pitts must have been so *tedious* for you. Though I am sure you thrived in your role," the Queen added jarringly.

Nushka forced a smile to her mouth that did not reach her eyes, her hair swaying back and forth behind her, betraying her attempt to appear composed.

"It was an honor to perform my duty, My Queen," Nushka forced herself to reply with saccharine sweetness, though the endearment made her want to vomit up her wine.

Beneath her feet, Zeri bristled on the floor in chimera form, picking up on Nushka's tense emotions. The creature had always been so intuitive, their two souls had been eternally bonded since its transformation.

"I only wish others had a chance to experience the fulfillment that such a role can bring," Nushka added, her tone sharp as a double-edged sword.

Aria was wise enough to appear mildly unnerved by her second comment, taking a long sip from her glass.

"Although…" Nushka continued sweetly, her sharp claws absentmindedly tapping on the goblet of wine in her hand, "I suppose that time has finally come. Do tell, who will my *lucky* replacement be? I hope they have thick skin and an even stronger stomach. Keeping millions of corrupt souls contained and overseeing their punishment is no easy task," she smiled, her claws lengthening around the glass she held.

Beneath the table, Zeri huffed in agreement. Bhoots were such intelligent and intuitive creatures. She tossed it a leg of meat beneath the table as a reward.

Growing up, Nushka had always preferred her mother over her father. However, she had long ago severed that familiar attachment. Nowadays they were only the King and Queen to her. Their role as Rulers was the only title she would acknowledge… and that was about to change should all go to plan. Nushka took another long drink of her wine.

The Goddess understood that Aria was mostly harmless, always choosing to see the good in others. Chiara, her sister, was a mirror image of the Queen in likeness and personality, hence why she was always their favorite and given the Afterworld to rule over. It was Archè that pulled Aria's marionette strings and, for that fact alone, Nushka thought she might spare her mother in the carnage. Perhaps sentencing her to rule over The Pitts would be a more fitting punishment for agreeing with her husband's plan to exile their own children. As for the King, he would likely find himself being Xanos's supper. Perhaps she would gift his heart to Hyacinth first. Nushka would be interested to see what, if any, of his magic then passed on to the magical beings.

Aria began answering her question, though immersed in her own thoughts, Nushka missed her reply and cursed herself for doing so. Unsure of how to respond, she simply nodded in agreement, hoping the action would suffice. She made a note to later ask Lilith who would take her place in The Pitts, however, it appeared she didn't need to wait.

Lilith rose, slamming her hands on the table.

"You cannot be serious!" she exclaimed, letting her temper slip, the afront startling the Queen and causing the King, who sat protectively by his wife's side, to narrow his eyes at her.

"Sit down, Lilith. We will discuss this later," Archè ordered, slamming his goblet of wine on the table. "We are here to celebrate. Be grateful that you are permitted to join us; there was no deal made with you. You will return and remain duty-bound guarding the Gate after the festivities are over."

Lilith's dark shadows shuddered furiously at the hem of her midnight ball gown, her eyes burning with liquid fury. The King's promise was exactly the kind of incentive Nushka needed to guarantee Lilith as an ally.

Thorn waltzed arrogantly into the room, shirtless despite the occasion and seated himself on the other side of Aria. It had been an age since Nushka had laid eyes on him. So carefree. She hoped that an eternity of playing war games, kept under her father's thumb, had not altered his character.

Apart from the occasional interaction with Lilith and now with the King and Queen, Nushka had not seen any of her kin since she was a youngling. She had not been visited by a single Deity in all her reign as Queen of Moor. Given she had refused their offers of visits early on in her reign, it had been at least a thousand years since a member of her family had requested to visit her realm.

An unfamiliar tightness stirred in Nushka's chest at the sight of her brother. They had played pranks together as younglings, delighting in their mischievous natures. But Lilith, at every turn, was there, thwarting their fun. Had things gone differently, Thorn and Nushka may have been close, had her heart not shriveled and the idea of affection and love had not become so abhorrent. Yet her chest tightened at the sight of him. She did not know what to make of the weakness, so instead of acknowledging the feeling any further, she downed the rest of her wine and then refilled her glass.

Thorn briefly made eye contact with Lilith and Nushka before pouring himself a glass of wine. He looked exactly as

Nushka remembered him, though slightly older, perhaps a little wiser. The resemblance between Archè and Thorn was uncanny.

"Greetings, Mother, Father, Sisters," he added with a wink. "My apologies for my tardiness. I had some time-sensitive *work* to attend to." He directed a reassuring nod to Archè that made the King of the Gods relax his shoulders a little.

"What have I missed?" Thorn asked casually, addressing no one in particular.

Aria's smile broadened at the sight of her son and she placed her hand upon his, giving it a gentle reassuring squeeze.

"You are just in time, my son. We have missed your company. We were just enjoying a late lunch before the festivities this evening," the Queen assured him sweetly.

The trill of her voice was a little higher than usual, a dead giveaway that she was hiding something from him. By the sudden tensing of Thorn's shoulders, he gathered as much too.

"Where is Chiara?" Nushka interrupted, suddenly aware her sister had not yet made her usual dramatic entrance.

Aria turned her attention towards her, obviously happy for the change of subject given her quickness to respond.

"Chiara is terribly busy; the Afterworld is practically bursting at the seams. She sends her apologies that she could not be here, but she will arrive in time to attend tonight's celebrations. What a delight it will be to have all my children in the same place for the first time since you were younglings," she cooed nostalgically, beaming with glee.

Beside her, Archè grunted his agreement as he took a sip of his own goblet. The King had hardly muttered a word all meal, their presence seemingly an inconvenience more than a joy.

"I see..." Nushka pondered, "and where is my ward? I would have thought she would be joining us... or are the deceased unworthy of a seat at your table?"

Archè raised a bow at her insinuation, and Nushka cursed herself for the slip of the tongue, reminding herself of the role she was meant to be playing. An act she was failing dismally at. Though perhaps revealing some of her true personality would also help convince them of her genuineness. The Rulers of the Gods may not be so keen to welcome someone who was wholly contrary to their memories. Such an act would have likely garnered their suspicion further.

"Agnes is resting and preparing for tonight's festivities in one of our guest suits. She is safe and comfortable, I assure you," Aria soothed her. "It was the King's idea. Such a magnanimous gesture of him, I think you'll agree." She batted her lashes adoringly towards her husband.

The sight almost made Nushka spit her wine, and the screeching of her claws on the glass momentarily resumed. Nushka forced herself to nod approvingly, while internally she began fretting that their plan had been ruined. Though, she rationalized to herself, if that were the case, she would likely be making small talk with the few Deities that resided in the prison of the Gods, rather than sipping on wine and pretending to play nice with her *family*.

Even still, Nushka gnawed on her lip. Archè would not blindly accept Agnes's redemption without further investigating the truth of it for himself. Perhaps that explained why Thorn was so late to the family meal. She had a feeling he had been enlisted to do the King's dirty work on more than one occasion. She scanned the King's and her brother's faces for any signs of their tells, but found none.

"Now that everyone is finally here, I believe it's time to eat," Archè announced, motioning with a flourish of his hand for the nymphs to begin serving their meal.

Platters of cold meats, fruits, cheeses, and fresh bread were brought out to graze upon for the first course. Followed by seasonal roast vegetables and a suckling pig which the King, to Nushka's surprise, carved himself. The Goddess of Blood and Bone would never stoop so low as to do such a menial task.

The nymphs made sure to keep the wine flowing—a fact that made managing her family's company entirely more tolerable. Dessert was Nushka's favorite; a platter of various cakes and a caramel fountain to dip fresh strawberries and other fruits into. It had been an age since she had tasted food so rich in flavor and so expertly prepared. The cooks in the castle of bone were all former mortal chefs who had been unfortunate enough to earn sentences to Moor. Their cooking was nothing compared to this. Nushka wasn't even sure if Lilith had staff on hand to prepare her meals for her. It had never occurred to her before now to ask. The Goddess of Darkness seemed to savor every bite as if in answer to Nushka's unasked question.

Only a full stomach could help to curb Nushka's temper at the stupidity of the whole gathering. The Royal family hadn't been together in eons and here they were pretending to play at happy families. Aria's behavior was suspiciously sweet, as if she thought one meal could make up for banishing her daughters to different realms for all eternity.

As conversation slowed and the meal drew toward its close, Archè excused himself from the table, claiming he wanted to rest before the night's entertainment. He insisted that Thorn escort him to his suite. Nushka had noticed the King's glazed eyes during the meal, his attention clearly elsewhere. Her shadows had whispered to her of his foot's incessant tapping beneath the table, the way his fingers twitched. Something was preoccupying his thoughts and it involved Thorn. Nushka was desperate to know if their plan was fated to end in disaster. If the King of the Gods was onto her, there was no chance of success.

Aria excused herself next, after first explaining that two of her own personal handmaidens would be in to escort the sisters to their guest suites and to help them prepare for the night ahead. Nushka insisted she would like to see her ward prior to retiring but Aria was quick to shut down the suggestion, again reassuring her that Agnes was safe and comfortable and that she would see her that evening. The possibility that Aria was deliberately keeping her ward from her caused Nushka further alarm.

Zeri pawed its way out from beneath the table to join them as the Goddess of Darkness and the Goddess of Blood and Bone rose from their seats.

"Leave us," Nushka said to the remaining staff waiting by the sides of the room.

A few of the nymphs seemed uneasy about the prospect of leaving the room unattended. The order no doubt contradicted some fundamental rule they were expected to abide, but they reluctantly did so anyway. None were stupid enough to risk earning either Deities' ire. They all knew exactly who Nushka and Lilith were and what they could do, even if many of the staff had never seen or met either of them before. The servants whispered; the halls could talk. No matter which realm you visited, gossip always travelled.

"Shall we?" Nushka offered Lilith a clawed hand.

When the room was finally clear, Lilith grasped her sister's outstretched hand and Zeri grasped a hold of its master's skirts. In a whir of Nushka's darkness, the Goddesses—Zeri in tow—left the spying eyes of The Land of the Gods and entered the scorching heat and chaos of The Pitts of Moor.

20

The Goddess of Darkness

The dry heat of The Pitts of Moor was unbearable. In all her long years of existence, Lilith had never encountered a more repulsive place. She instantly regretted the voluminous evening gown she wore, but with a flick of her hand the multiple layers of tulle beneath her silk skirt disappeared, floating away into the ether. The realm was not a place for ballgowns and tiaras, but the long-lived Deity would never stoop to wearing anything more practical. Her clothes were her armor after all.

Smoke and ash hung in the air, sending Lilith into a coughing fit. How Nushka had endured living in such an abhorrent realm for so long, deprived of fresh air, she could not fathom. Side-by-side the Goddesses stood at the entrance to a towering castle of bone. The Goddess had never beheld Nushka's seat of power before, and she couldn't help the shiver that rippled over her skin at the sight.

Spread out across the volcanic plains, seemingly immune to the conditions, was the Goddess of Blood and Bone's gathered army. Peuchen flew in formation on dragon wings of deepest purple, their barbed tails flowing ominously behind them. A herd of chimera gathered at the base of The Pitt's jagged mountains. Smog and noxious gases filled the air, making it difficult to breathe or gauge the size of the herd.

Lilith requested on several occasions to visit her sister in Moor, but her requests had always been rejected. Nushka had been so angry at the universe, and the Rulers of the Gods for the fate that had been bestowed upon her, that she had denied anyone outside of her wicked circle access to the realm.

The Goddess of Darkness's own work was never-ending, and as time drifted by, and each attempt to contact her sister failed, she had mentally closed the door on their relationship. The next time Lilith saw Nushka had been in her own realm. She was even more lost to the Gods than she had been before her sentence by that stage. Hardly a trace of the youngling Lilith had known and grown up with could be seen.

As the years passed by, the only time the sisters were reunited was when Nushka would deem to grace Lilith with her presence, always when attempting to invoke the rule of redemption. Of course, none of the souls that Nushka brought before Lilith were by any means good or repentant. Thus, the dance Lilith and Nushka performed together grew tiresome and the sisters grew further apart. Just as Aria and Archè had likely intended.

Each time Nushka tried deceiving her, Lilith could not fathom why her sister was so intent to give up her responsibilities and return to the coddled Land of the Gods. After finally seeing The Pitts for herself, Lilith fully comprehended her sister's dire circumstances, and a small knot of guilt started twisting in her stomach.

The bone gates of the castle entrance creaked open on a phantom wind, and through them Hyacinth, leader of the wendigast coven, began making her way towards them. Zeri quirked its ears at the sound and watched on curiously at their master's side as the High Witch approached.

Hyacinth's gangly limbs and long spider-silk hair reminded Lilith of creatures of old, in another universe long since traversed. The last time she had encountered such creatures was eons before her parents had begun creating the mortal realms in this universe. Part tree spirit and part witch; they were no more trustworthy than the creator who stood by her side. Lilith wondered how many of their species awaited inside the confines of the castle, readying to cast their wicked magic upon her kin. No doubt they had a slew of devastating potions brewed and packaged neatly in glass vials, ready to use at a moment's notice.

Their magic was different to that of the Gods. As the wendigast species were descendants of Nushka, a drop of her dark blood magic flowed through their veins. With the ability to wield nature to their will, the combination of the two magics had devastating effects. Of all the creatures that gathered in Nushka's dark army, it was the wendigast that Lilith respected.

On Nushka's signal, a bone horn sounded from one of the soaring turrets—a summons. A chorus of horns relayed the call, echoing one after the next, summoning one and all. Even those in the far reaches of The Pitts were called to make their way to the Queen of Moor's seat of power. A signal that war would soon be upon them.

The ground beneath the Goddesses' feet began to shudder, as hundreds of her sister's followers began making the journey towards them. Screeches and roars filled the air. Each warrior, regardless of species or race, was eager for blood and vengeance. Zeri redirected their attention away from Hyacinth's approach and began bounding around in anticipation of the approaching herd of chimera. It warmed Lilith's heart to see her sister bonded with such a loyal beast, even if Nushka would deny holding any affection for the pet.

Hyacinth approached Nushka's side and dipped her head in reverence. Lilith noted how the High Witch had replaced her traditional garb of the tree spirit witches with thick, leather-plated armor. Only once before could Lilith recall seeing the female dress as such. That day, the immortal had wiped out half of her own clan to cement her title and claim her crown as High Witch. Lilith had watched the entire ruthless event play out through her clouded visions. Today, Lilith supposed, the wendigast leader hoped to claim a new crown for her master.

"My Queen," Hyacinth addressed Nushka, who paid her no heed, her attention elsewhere. "The wendigast are ready in the Hall. We march at your command."

Nushka nodded.

"The plan is in motion," the Queen of Moor replied. "Once I have activated your potion, I will open a portal between the two realms. You and your kin will lead the charge into the banquet hall during the ball. Bind as many of the Deities with your magic as you can. My remaining followers will deal with the rest."

"As you wish, My Queen," Hyacinth bowed before taking her leave back into the castle.

Lilith stepped up to her sister's side once more.

"Is this your whole army?" she questioned. "After all your talk, I had expected more…" the Goddess of Darkness smirked.

Nushka met her banter with a wicked grin of her own.

"Perhaps once Ilbis and his descendants arrive, you will be more impressed, dear sister," she goaded.

Surprise flared in Lilith's emerald eyes.

"It has been an age since I have heard that name… He still serves you then?" Lilith enquired. She could not help the tinge of awe in her voice.

Ilbis was such a strange and powerful being, so incredibly unique. He was by far the Goddess of Blood and Bone's greatest creation. She had imagined Ilbis had become so powerful in his own right that Nushka had lost control of his leash eons ago. Apparently, she was wrong.

"He pushes my limits at every opportunity, I assure you. But at the end of the day, he does not forget who holds his reins. Even if he did, he would be no match for me," Nushka boasted, her hair whipping behind her frantically.

"I'm sure that is likely the case…" Lilith conceded. "But do you think it wise to unleash him, given his unpredictability?"

"Perhaps not," Nushka confessed to Lilith's surprise. "But I do not think he will betray me."

"Betray *us*?" Lilith clarified with a raised eyebrow.

Nushka's grin grew wider, more feral. "Of course, my sister," she replied condescendingly. "I do not think he will betray *us*."

Lilith was less than convinced, but if he did turn on her, she was sure she could deal with him. Unless he used his unique skillset on her first. Lilith reinforced her mental shields as a precaution.

Before a never-ending wave of all manner of wicked beasts, the two Deities watched the great army draw nearer, the sound of their collective marching rising as they approached the castle. Zeri became frenzied with excitement as its spiritual kin of sorts pressed nearer.

The flapping of the mighty peuchens' wings sounded like cannon booms. The gusts from their wings thankfully managed to clear away some of the smog as they came to land, the army assembling on the other side of the bone castle's draw bridge. The whole castle was surrounded by an impressive moat of lava.

Ilbis strolled cockily out of the castle bone gates, the ground trembling beneath his feet. Power radiated off him, and hundreds of ghoul offspring trailed him. Their significant numbers amazed the Goddess of Darkness. Mandigon, and his clan of edimmu with their characteristic blue tinged skin and fiery red eyes, traversed closely at their heels.

The Demi-God Ilbis offered Lilith a curt nod as he passed her on his way to join the gathered army, the ghouls and edimmu following his lead. The wendigast would not be joining them for Nushka's grand speech, Lilith realized. The lava of the plains likely made the tree spirits apprehensive; the Goddess did not blame them.

'Every being has its weakness, even those with hearts as black as night.'

The Queen of Moor ascended the steps overlooking the plains and her people, readying to deliver her address. Lilith took in the ebony figure-hugging gown her sister wore and the imposing crown of bone now perched upon her head. Whom the bones had belonged to, Lilith didn't want to know, nor did she particularly care. She had her own bone collection. Their menacing impact was long lost on her, but Lilith could see how her sister's followers would lap up the crown. Not just a Queen of The Pitts, but a conqueror of death.

With a barely perceptible nod in her pet's direction, Nushka gave Zeri permission to join the herd of chimera that paced at the front of the army. It would no doubt be fighting by their sides in the upcoming battle.

Nushka, Queen of Moor and all wicked beings, raised her arms and the dark army stilled.

"The time has come, tonight we strike!" The Queen of Moor declared. "Our plan is underway and soon our enemy will be vulnerable! Hyacinth and her wendigast will lead the charge. Ilbis will follow next with his subjects. Then Mandigon and the edimmu."

"Peuchen," Nushka continued. "I want you circling the castle in the sky. Kill any who try to escape. Chimera, you are my final surprise weapon. Gather or rip apart any who try to flee. All of you should offer our enemy a *brief* opportunity to surrender. If they do not, then you have authority to use your gifts upon them or kill on sight. Tonight, we will live like Gods!" the Goddess of Blood and Bone decreed.

The army roared in delight and Lilith's stomach dropped. The orders Nushka gave were vastly different from those they had discussed. This would not simply be an invasion, but an annihilation.

The Queen of Moor turned from her raptly cheering army and returned to her sister's side, mischief gleaming in her fiery gaze. Her claws outstretched, ready for a fight, her hair a writhing, living thing behind her.

"No Deity is meant to be harmed unless absolutely necessary!" Lilith confronted her sister furiously when she was within earshot, nostrils flared.

The Goddess of Darkness struggled to rein in the shadows threatening to break free and attack any that opposed their master's wishes. They, too, demanded justice.

"Don't be so naïve, Lilith, this is war. Deities will die, whether you wish it so or not," Nushka stated matter-of-factly, teeth gleaming menacingly. "You need to remember that even though we are allies, this is my army, not yours, and I will wield it as I see fit."

'Thorn… Chiara… My family… I want to be Queen but I don't want them dead! Nushka is going too far…'

Lilith's cheeks heated, her fingers curled, shadows ready to pounce.

"Why would you give your followers free rein to kill and torment whoever they please?! What about our family?" Lilith screamed. "That was not the plan we agreed upon and you know it! Why are you so willing to go back on your word and shed blood so thoughtlessly?"

Lilith's power thrummed furiously beneath her skin, preparing to defend herself if need be.

She was fooling herself, thinking her sister could have changed. Of course Nushka would command her subjects to kill without consequence, preferring to take down her enemy by any means rather than valuing life. The punitive approach was the *only* approach as far as Nushka would ever be concerned. The alliance they shared was based on mutual distaste for their situations, it did not make them any more alike than they were before.

"And why in your right mind would you allow me to witness this betrayal?!" Lilith's eyes widened in disbelief. She knew the answer before the words were out of her mouth.

Nushka bared her teeth in a cruel smile, her eyes alight with the promise of bloodshed.

"This speech was not just an order to your followers, but also a warning... A test. For me," she breathed.

"Yes, it was... and you failed," Nushka replied ominously. "I do not have time to convince you the path you wish to follow is wrong, so I will just have to take matters into my own hands."

With a quick flourish of her magic, Nushka forced Lilith to the ground and bound her limbs with shadow magic. With another curl of her hand, she summoned Ilbis to her side, his eyes instantly trained upon her.

"Please, don't do this Nushka! We are a team! We want the same things!" Lilith begged her, desperately trying and failing to break out of the magical bindings that restrained her. She lashed at the bindings with her own shadow power, but Nushka's shadows kept squeezing her tighter.

Nushka's returning cackle was a thing of nightmares. Despite Lilith's mental defenses, Ilbis attacked her with his enhanced mind conqueror gifting, penetrating through each layer with a slash of his telekinetic claws, eviscerating her mental shields. Ilbis crushed her shields quicker than Lilith could re-build them. She clenched her teeth against the pain of his intrusion, eyes screwed shut in concentration as she fought against his telepathic attack. A moment later, her eyes glazed over, and she slumped temporarily unconscious.

Several minutes later, Lilith roused on the hard slate floor of the bone castle entrance, a sudden bloodlust coursing through her veins.

Lilith rose from the ground on unsteady feet, her wrists and ankles strangely sore, nausea roiled in her stomach. She wiped her dirty hands on her skirts to remove the dust.

"Nushka? Ilbis? Why was I on the floor? What am I doing in The Pitts?" She asked, noticing the unfamiliar surroundings.

The intense heat assaulted Lilith's eyes and nose, something she was sure she could never grow accustomed to. Nushka offered her sister an unnervingly tranquil smile.

"My darling sister, you fainted," Nushka reassured her. "I suspect the heat got the better of you. We were just rallying the host, readying to attack the Land of the Gods."

Lilith's nerves eased at the reassurance, though she could not recall arriving in Moor at all. Slowly, plans of the invasion resurfaced, and her stomach unfurled with relief.

We will destroy our parent's legacy; we will take the seat of power that is owed to us. We will do whatever it takes, even kill, to achieve our means.' The thoughts swirled around in her mind like a revolving door.

Lilith looked at a smug Ilbis, wary of the slight satisfaction gracing his features.

'Why can't I remember fainting or arriving here? What have they done to me?' Lilith despaired.

Lilith assessed her mental shields, but they were intact. Before feelings of concern could take root, they were replaced with a sense of peacefulness and comfort. Another rush of emotion urged her to trust Nushka, who had never led her astray before. The Dark Goddess allowed the soothing feelings to consume her, washing away any doubt. Even her shadows calmed at her feet, and all wariness or suspicion floated away.

The Goddess of Blood and Bone

Through a portal of darkness, Lilith and Nushka re-entered the formal dining room located in the Rulers' castle in the Land of the Gods. Two of Aria's handmaidens awaited their return. This time, Zeri did not follow them. Her pet was content to play with the chimera herd, and Nushka did not begrudge it that enjoyment. They would be reunited in battle soon enough.

Lilith radiated unease, her shoulders stiff. Nushka worried that Ilbis may not have been skilled enough to fully manipulate her sister's mind. Initially, it had seemed to work; Lilith had not questioned Nushka again regarding her intentions for the Deities residing in the Land of the Gods. But now, Nushka was not so sure...

After a quick glance of apprehension towards her sister, Lilith followed the handmaiden that had been assigned to take her to her quarters. If the servants suspected anything amiss from their brief disappearance, they did not let it show.

A wraith, who introduced herself as Clythia, began leading the Goddess of Blood and Bone to her own guest suite. To her dismay, they headed in the opposite direction to Lilith, which made Nushka wary. A gentle breeze caused her silk gown and shadows to flutter as they walked.

The Goddess was eager to find out what had happened to Agnes since her arrival, and to make sure that her plan had not been spoiled by the incompetent wretched soul. Nushka sent her shadows creeping around the floors and walls as they walked, searching for signs of her handmaiden. After scaling one flight of stairs, then another, Nushka grinded her teeth as she continued to follow Aria's servant blindly through the halls.

As a youngling, her bedroom had been on this floor, and feelings of nostalgia took her by surprise as she eagerly looked for the door. Though, eons later, she reasoned that the suite had likely changed hands hundreds of times.

The Dark Goddess's shadows became frantic as the familiar scent of ash and fire assailed her as they went to pass another door. Without a second thought, she stopped trailing the servant. Unsurprisingly, the door was locked. A flare of her dark magic had the door blasted off its hinges and landing with a heavy thud on the suite floor.

Seated comfortably at a dressing table facing away from her, clad in a gown of deep red silk, Agnes was having her golden hair styled into loose curls by a nymph. Blood red lipstick shone on her lips, and the thought of what those lips and that mouth could do had warmth pooling in the Goddess's core. She cursed her thoughts. The girl before her was merely a pawn, she would do well to remember it.

Agnes's eyes flew to hers through the mirror's reflection as she pursed her lips.

"Leave us," Nushka commanded from the doorway.

The timid water nymph scampered out of the room through a back-servant's entrance, giving Nushka as wide a birth as possible. With cautious calculation, Agnes's eyes darted around the room, seemingly checking for exits.

Nushka cast a stream of her shadows around the room, coating every surface and blocking every entry from prying eyes and ears. The room transformed from a light and airy sanctuary into a black abyss, the only light coming from a scented candle that burned by the bedside.

Agnes rose from a stool and turned to face the Goddess, only a few strides separating them. The tension was so thick it could be cut with a knife. The handmaiden was devastatingly beautiful, though it pained the Goddess to admit it. Her cheeks were rosy from layers of make-up the nymph had applied. After all they had shared together, all that Agnes had done for her, Nushka often forgot that she was no longer living and her body… it was no more real than the moment they shared in the hot springs. That day felt like a lifetime ago, and yet she could still feel the pebble of Agnes's skin beneath her touch, could still imagine the feel of her tongue within her, tasting her.

Nushka shook her head to clear her thoughts, reminding herself of the task at hand.

"Did you achieve your mission?" Nushka asked with her arms crossed, claws extended.

Agnes's gaze turned sharp. "If you are feeling thirsty tonight, I would not drink the wine," she snapped.

A moment of surprise crossed Nushka's face, and she allowed a small, wicked smirk to form. "You have held up your end of the bargain, Agnes."

The use of her name on Nushka's lips felt sour, too personal for what they shared, what they were to each other—nothing. This was a business arrangement, nothing more, she reminded herself. Though she doubted she would hold up her own end of the bargain. As far as Nushka was concerned, the handmaiden should be grateful for every moment she was allowed in her presence. This strange attachment she felt towards Agnes, it was dangerous. It threatened all she believed in. To feel was to be weak and she would *not* be weak. After her coup was over, she would put the handmaiden back in her place.

"You sound surprised," Agnes rolled her eyes. "The Queen of the Gods invited me for tea..." Agnes added after a moment, returning to her seat when she realized Nushka would not approach her.

Nushka lip curled baring her teeth. "What did Aria want?!"

"She wanted dirt on you." Agnes picked at her nails, her mouth drawing into a smirk. "Her method was surprising, though her questions were not. But don't worry, I told her nothing. She still thinks me a meek and mild weakling who only wants forgiveness for her past crimes. She has no idea of the predator lurking beneath my skin."

Amusement crossed Nushka's face. The girl had balls, the Goddess would give her that.

"Good," Nushka replied, her mouth pulling into a tight-lipped smile.

'Here's the woman demanding my attention. The soul with fire in her heart.'

The thought crossed her mind before Nushka had a chance to squelch it, and she mentally chastised herself.

'Weak. That is what I will become if Agnes remains in my service. I don't know why she affects me so. I never had this problem with any of my other handmaidens. She needs to go,' Nushka thought repulsively.

The Goddess of Blood and Bone shuddered, her shadows withdrawing to her. She turned on her heels and left the room. Nushka had all the information she needed. The plan was still on track. She didn't need any more distractions, and Agnes was the epitome of distraction. She needed distance between them. If she stayed in that suite any longer, staring at her in that tantalizing red dress, those perfectly painted red lips, she knew it would only end in trouble. Agnes was a threat she needed to rid herself of. The handmaiden had served her purpose, and now Nushka needed to discard her or risk coming to care for her. The thought sent another shiver down Nushka's spine.

Clythia waited for her in the hallway. As soon as Nushka rejoined her, she silently resumed her tour, leading the Dark Goddess three doors down the corridor, to her former suite as a youngling. The suite was exactly as she had left it all those eons ago.

22

Agnes

The banquet hall in the castle reminded Agnes of the great hall back in Castle Brandistone. A large balcony surrounded the room on three sides, trailing out into the open air from the archways encompassing the room.

Candles floated above the Deities as day turned to night, and it reminded Agnes of home, when her sisters would have lit them with their fire-wielding giftings. The immortals danced to ancient songs performed by a stringed quartet who played with a precision only an immortal's lifespan could produce. Their craft was so honed, the music was an extension of themselves; a shedding of skin to bare their souls to those blessed to hear their melodies. Such details hadn't held her interest in her human life, but her wretched experience in Moor had caused her to seek out such beauty, to appreciate it with fresh ears.

Aria and Archè had not yet arrived, evidenced by their empty thrones upon the dais erected on the far side of the expansive room. Agnes saw no sign of either the Goddess of Darkness or the Goddess of Blood and Bone. Relief filled her as she realized she was free to enjoy the celebrations, no matter how briefly. She had not allowed herself to consider it was even an option.

Surrounded by a hall of predators, Agnes felt helpless without a weapon. In her mortal life she had always strapped a dagger to her thigh for protection. Though such an object would have been impossible to conceal tonight. The deep red gown clung to her every curve before draping softly to the ground.

Dressed in a gown of such finery, hair styled, and make-up applied to perfection, Agnes drifted towards the dance floor, the music drawing her in. A waiter passed her along the way, offering her a glass of wine which she eagerly went to accept, but then quickly realized her mistake and left the glass upon the tray. A small, curious spark lit the waiter's gaze, but he shrugged it off and continued moving throughout the room, tray of crystal glasses balanced perfectly on one hand.

Agnes resumed her graceful walk towards the dance floor where couples danced lovingly, arm-in-arm, their love and light flowing from them like an aura. A soft blanket of clouds whimsically shrouded the floor.

"Excuse my interruption, madam," a husky accented voice sounded from behind her, "but it seems I find myself without a dance partner and you look as though you have need of one too. Could I trouble you for a dance?"

Thorn.

A smile curved her lips. The God of War was dressed to perfection for the evening's event, though unlike her, he had likely managed to conceal a small arsenal of weapons beneath his garments.

"Are you lost?" she taunted, raising an eyebrow. "You must be, to have sought me out amongst all the beauties in this room." She gestured around her with a flourish to emphasize the point.

Thorn's returning smile was predatory, his gaze ravenous as he surveyed her in the gown he had adorned her with earlier. Agnes felt butterflies flutter around her stomach.

"Now where would the fun be in that?" he teased, pulling her into the crowd of dancers before she could object.

Thorn's warm hand weighed heavily at her waist, his other finding her hand, and so they waltzed. Thorns steps were light as a feather from years of combat training. Agnes herself moved with the grace of a swan as years of dance training as a Princess flooded back to her. Hours flew by as Agnes lost herself to the music in the arms of the God of War. The magic of this realm pulsed though her, coaxing her to unleash herself, urging her to cast aside all concerns. Her head became light from exhilaration, her feet seeming to float on air. Why the God had chosen to dance with her, Agnes couldn't understand. Morbid curiosity, perhaps? Whatever it was, she was grateful for it.

The God of War's muscular chest pressed against her own, his hand wandering dangerously close to her behind. More than once, she had wondered what it would feel like to bed him—not to make love. She wanted to fuck him until she saw stars, pure carnal need overcoming her. An urge so compelling she wanted to rip the blasted God's pants off where he stood. Sensing her rising need, Thorn pulled her in closer, until one subtle movement would have had their lips exploring each other.

"It's the music," Thorn whispered in her ear, as if that were explanation enough. "It's an aphrodisiac in our realm. The instruments are infused with the Goddess of Love's power. As the musicians play, those that hear its seductive melody are filled with *want*." His voice emphasized the last word.

Heat curled in Agnes's core, and she found herself writhing, wanting any kind of friction between her legs. She needed him, wanted the feel of him in her hand, lusting for the taste of him.

Agnes drew her gaze away from Thorn, needing to distract herself from the overpowering feelings. No longer were couples dancing so innocently in the firelight. Hands searched, limbs were entangled, and lips explored as the floor became less of a dance floor and more like the primal gatherings during Nushka's evening entertainment. The Deities were lost to the trance of the music and their baser urges.

"Do you dare to answer the music's call?" Thorn whispered boldly, and Goddess curse her she did.

Agnes wanted to experience all of it. If tonight could be her last night in this form or any other, she needed to know what it would feel like to be with him—to feel him.

Heat flared in her eyes. "I think the question is why do *you* dare, prince? After all, I am damaged goods," she snapped, though there was no anger behind her words.

Thorn's gaze smoldered. Her breathing hitched as he leaned in closer, his breath gently caressing her ear.

"Since I am about to be damned to The Pitts for aiding in your scheme, I figure I may as well enjoy myself before my life and the realm goes to hell," he whispered fiendishly.

His words sent shivers down her spine. Agnes's bold grin was all the answer Thorn needed, as his gaze slowly raked over every inch of her in that stunning gown. He entangled one callused hand in her wavy locks, the other roving over her hips and finally finding its home at her rear. Everywhere he touched felt like the answer to some ungodly prayer.

Not able to hold back any longer, Agnes unleashed herself upon him, losing herself to the music. Their mouths touched and electricity kindled within her core. Their kisses were an assault, a frenzy of teeth and tongues. Tasting, exploring. The hardness of him pressed against the front of her dress right where she needed him as they drew even closer.

Slowly, they danced towards the edge of the room, their limbs entwined as they swayed and explored each other's bodies, their lips never parting. The music seemed to make everything else fall away, heightening their focus on each other. Only their touch and the feel of each other mattered. Their senses of need and want overcoming all rational thought. Heat flooded Agnes's core as Thorn lifted her into the air, and she wrapped her legs around his waist, causing her dress to split up to the thigh. She did not care in the slightest.

The God of War carried her out of the great banquet hall with such inconceivable gentleness, she might have believed he cared for her in some soul-deep way. They crossed through an ornate archway into the darkness of the balcony, with only the firelight seeping from the hall and the full moon's radiant light to guide their way.

Countless stars twinkled around them in the night sky, their clear, vibrant glow a mesmerizing sight to behold. Around the balcony's edge wove a waist-high railing covered with vines of night blooming blossoms. Thorn delicately rested Agnes atop the railing.

The God slowly withdrew his soft lips from hers to take in the view of her perched like a Goddess amongst the clouds, her hair nearly glowing in the moonlight.

"Magnificent," he breathed in that husky accent, making her knees weak.

Agnes pulled him closer once more, craving the feel of his skin pressed against her own. She was hungry for his touch. Not willing to wait any longer, she leaned forward and began greedily untying his tight black leather pants, before wrapping a hand around the hard silken length of him. The God released a moan of pleasure, his power rippling off him in a wave of ecstasy. The size of him took her breath away. If she had still been human, she wasn't sure she would have been able to handle him.

Thorn leaned into her touch, moving in turn with her hand as she slid up and down the length of him. His lips and teeth found her neck and devoured her. The God's rough hand began exploring her breast. The feel of her peaked nipples and the tight, quick pulsing of her hand drew another primal moan from the God, echoing her own as she leaned into his touch.

A wall of cyclonic dark wind raised around them, blocking them from prying eyes. The God of War grasped her waist and lowered her from the balcony. He fell to his knees and took his time as he hitched the slightly damp skirt of her gown.

The sight of the God knelt before her was breathtaking. Thorn treated her with a reverence she was not used to, and it tugged on her few remaining heartstrings, forging her anew. He took his time with her, feasting upon her, drawing out her pleasure and savoring her. His tongue explored her, teasingly enough that she couldn't help but grab fistfuls of his hair and urge him on. She writhed against his fingers and the roguish tongue that drew such gloriously sinful sensations from her. He worshipped her in such a way she never wanted it to end.

Agnes had never felt such desire and indulgence, had never been treated with such care and affection. She had never connected with anyone like this before. The way she was bullied and felt unloved as a child, had caused her to build a wall around her emotions to protect herself from being hurt. Here with Thorn, she felt those walls starting to breakdown as a flood of emotions washed over her. She could give affection and receive it freely in return. Agnes did not feel so cold and empty anymore. With Thorn, she felt wanted rather than used.

Agnes moaned as she leaned into Thorn's touch. She had never felt so on the verge of teetering over the edge in ecstasy; she couldn't imagine ever experiencing such immense pleasure again. She relished every moment, delighting in the frenzy and the exquisite feel of him.

As he rose from his knees, the wall of wind raging around them, he not-so-gently turned her around, one hand fisted in her skirts, the other hand wrapped around her front so he could grasp her firm breasts again as he plummeted inside her.

She saw stars as pure decadence flooded her core. Only this mattered, only their joining. In and out, the steady thrum of him inside of her. She needed more of him, needed all of him; the heat and desire growing within her begging for release.

The God of War moaned in frustration, wanting full access to her, the tightly fitted gown depriving him of her. With a whisper of his dark power, her gown fizzled into a stream of smoke, leaving her utterly bare before him. He released an appreciative groan as he continued adoring her breasts, worshipping her behind, and fucking her as if she were the only thing in the universe that mattered.

Leaning forward, one hand steadying her against the railing, her free fingers explored that spot just above where his cock thrusted inside her. Massaging that bundle of nerves her breathing turned to rasps.

"Holy rutting Gods," she moaned.

The feeling of him pressed against her skin was the only thing keeping her tethered to the universe. Faster and faster, he pulsed inside her. With each stroke he pushed deeper within her as she continued to revel in her own touch. Excruciating pleasure washed through her burning her from the inside out.

Without warning, Thorn withdrew from her fully, spinning her around so she was facing him and lifting her gently back onto the rail. She bunched her hands in his gloriously thick and wavy hair. A bead of sweat trickled down his brow and trailed down his now bare chest. When he had taken his shirt off, she couldn't recall. She stared at him, in awe at the tight muscles, the dip in his abdomen that led to his hard length, promising more to come. She greedily drank in the sight of him.

The God of War slid back inside her. With one hand he resumed exploring her breasts, while the other dropped precariously low, until he found that sensitive bundle of nerves she had just been tending to and drew out her pleasure. Thorn massaged that spot in such a way that made Agnes gasp, and this time she was sure there was no coming back from such an experience as this. He would ruin sex for her. It would never feel as good again as it did right now, she was sure of it.

She thanked the stars, rather than the Gods, for granting her this one moment, this one damn moment, where nothing else mattered but her and the God before her. He elicited sounds from her that Agnes hadn't even known were possible.

Onward he thrust, faster and faster, harder and harder. The pressure inside her so strong she thought she might tear in two from ecstasy. With one final thrust, they both found their pleasure, Thorn moaning and Agnes releasing a scream of undiluted joy. He rolled his hips into her hers, slower and slower, drawing out that moment, the incomparable sensation. Her head lolled back, her eyes fluttering closed as she enjoyed every wave of contentment that washed over her.

She couldn't imagine returning to living a life so emotionally closed off as she had before today. The walls she had built over the years in her mind had thoroughly shattered and she never wanted to go back to that dark, lonely way of existing ever again.

After he finally stilled within her, Agnes lifted her head and they caught each other's gaze, heat smoldering in their eyes. The music floating outside seemed to release a sigh of relief that its call had been answered.

Shoulders back, Thorn's lips pulled into a smug smile of satisfaction as he withdrew from her. Agnes quirked her eyebrow, daring him to voice whatever cocky thought was running through his mind. But he held back, as if he too did not want to ruin the moment, as if their joining had been just as life-altering for him as it had been for her.

With a flick of the God of War's power, he was redressed and Agnes was dressed again in an exact replica of the deep red silk gown she had worn before he had turned it into ash and smoke.

"Of all the dresses you could have magicked up, you recreated this one. Why?" she asked genuinely curious.

His face softened as he gazed upon her with such adoration that she felt unworthy.

"Because the way you look in that dress, makes me want to fall at my knees and worship you over and over again. You are beautiful Agnes, inside and out."

He spoke with such conviction and kindness that it took her breath away. She blushed, tears welling in her eyes. She gave him a small, genuine smile and threw her arms around him. He hugged her in return. Even if the realm was about to go to hell, as Thorn put it, they would still have this untainted, blissful memory.

23

The God of War

Beneath the moonlight, Thorn marveled at the woman he held. He had meant every word he had said.

"That damn dress," he breathed breaking the tension.

Agnes huffed a laugh and pulled away from their embrace.

Thorn couldn't believe how far he had allowed things to go. Allowing himself to fall prey to the power of the music, fucking her as he did. He had been reckless for so many reasons. He had worshipped her as though she were the only woman that had and ever would matter to him. He sighed.

The God of War would never admit it outright, but he knew it was always going to end that way. The moment he pinned her to the floor in the suite and she smirked back at him in challenge, he knew he had finally met his match. And that wicked, awful mouth of hers...

"Holy rutting Moor, I am in such deep shit," he moaned, finally dropping the tunnel of wind around them, revealing them once more to anyone venturing out onto the balcony.

Judging by Agnes's returning gaze, she seemed inclined to agree, but he beheld not a single ounce of regret in that piercing gaze. She had enjoyed herself just as much as he had; he knew that based on the sweet moans of satisfaction he'd elicited from her—a thought that boosted his ego to no end.

The way she looked at him now and he at her, gave him goosebumps He had never felt that connected to anyone before. He didn't know what that meant and now was not the time to overanalyze his feelings given the chaos that was shortly to ensure.

Those full red lips and those glorious breasts framed perfectly in that gown still taunted him. It took all his self-control not to whisk her away to his suite and see what else that mischievous mouth of hers could do.

Then he felt *her* approach...

"Fuck!" Thorn cursed, turning abruptly from Agnes to face his youngest sister as she neared.

Dressed in an elegant shimmering golden gown, much like the one their mother Aria had worn to lunch, Chiara, the Goddess of Light, dazzled like a ray of sunshine.

"Hello darling brother of mine," she smiled. "It has been an age."

She pulled him into a hug, pressing a soft kiss to his cheek. Thorn kissed her brow in return, before pulling out from her embrace to look her over. Chiara hadn't changed at all since he had last seen her. Still lovely as always. The Goddess of Light was the personification of decency, having remained untainted by corrupt immortals. Though he was sure she had grown wiser to the ways of the universe—it was impossible not to. Even confined to the Afterworld, granting 'happily-ever-afters' to deserving souls, he was sure she had learned a thing or two about the ways of the many realms.

"You're looking radiant, sister," he said with a warm smile. "The Afterworld must be treating you well. How have you been?"

At this point he knew he would say and do anything to distract his sister from the guest he was obviously trying—and failing miserably—to conceal behind him.

"I am wonderful, as always. The Afterworld keeps me busy. It is a thankless job, oh wait—no it isn't!" She teased with a wink. "Of course, all my subjects adore me and I them."

Thorn nodded his head in understanding, though the idea of anyone worshipping him for any reason other than to request victory and protection on the battlefield was a wholly unfamiliar concept.

"I was just heading back to the ball. Would you care to join me, sister?" Thorn asked a little too obviously, offering her his arm, but Chiara was having none of it and pushed past him, heading straight for Agnes.

Chiara raked her gaze over Agnes through fluttering eye lashes.

"Well, look who we have here," she leaned forward placing a hand over her heart. "The lady of the hour. The soul who appeared to not only redeem my sister's heart, but who has also stolen the heart of my brother it seems."

She grinned at them both. Thorn froze. There was no avoiding the conversation then. He waited to see how it would all play out and prayed Agnes turned on that hidden charm that had won him over.

"You must be a prize indeed…" Chiara trilled, the sound unnervingly like their mother.

Agnes had the good sense to bow for the Goddess before thanking her for her kind words. Chiara approached Agnes and surveyed her like a hawk.

"Of course, I didn't think such a task could be achieved," Chiara hummed in that annoying way Thorn was used to her doing as a child.

Thorn had always hated the way Chiara drew out her musings rather than cutting to the point. His sister enjoyed dangling pieces of information over people, toying with them before her grand reveal.

"With all due respect, Goddess, I'm not sure what you mean… What didn't you think could be achieved?" Agnes replied as she fidgeted with her fingers.

Chiara's eyes sparkled, her answering grin startling.

"I am referring to your miraculous redemption, of course," Chiara replied, her smile crinkling her eyes. "I must admit that I still find it rather hard to believe, I'm afraid. *Especially* after meeting with your family in the Afterworld."

'Oh fuck.' Thorn wasn't sure he was breathing. He had taken on fierce armies in his life. He had faced off against his father on multiple occasions, but Chiara—he had not expected this from her of all people. If she suspected anything, their whole plan could be ruined.

"That was, of course, why I couldn't be here to join you for lunch," Chiara continued, laying out the breadcrumbs as she liked to do. "I felt it was my duty to speak with your family to see if they believed your change of conscience was possible. Like obtaining a character reference. I must admit that your father, Titian, was less than convinced. As for your mother, Amealiana, she was hopeful. A mother always sees the best in her children, even the wretched ones. It was Annie, surprisingly, that strongly advocated for you. Though she sees the good in all people, so unfortunately her opinion carries little weight."

Tears welled in Agnes's eyes at the mention of her family. But she schooled her features and donned the mask she wore like armor. Thorn had to admit the girl was tough. She had to have been to have survived The Pitts for so long.

Agnes ran a hand threw her hair as she took a slow deep breath.

"Thank you for speaking with them. Many a time I have wondered how they still feel about me," Agnes spoke softly and sincerely. Her shoulders slumped as she sighed. "I know that I have caused them harm, and for that I am deeply sorry. I want to be reunited with them so I can seek their forgiveness. I assure you, Goddess, my intentions are honorable. I just want a second chance to change my ways," Agnes claimed with another bow of her head.

Thorn felt the truth in her words and it surprised him. She wasn't perfect, she had done inconceivable things to those closest to her, but she was trying to change. She was trying to better herself. There was something so refreshingly unique about her that had him thoroughly ensnared in her web.

Chiara twisted her mouth crinkling her nose.

"We'll see..." she murmured, eyeing her suspiciously.

Thorn gave Agnes a small smile he hoped conveyed that he believed her, even though Chiara didn't. He saw her soul and he did not recoil from it, not anymore.

Then Chiara turned back to Thorn. Her frown replaced unnervingly easily with her usual warm, hopeful smile. Chiara clapped gleefully like a giddy schoolgirl.

"I hear congratulations are in order on your promotion!" For once Thorn had no idea what she was talking about, but her enthusiasm had him on high alert.

"Out with it, Chiara," he grumbled folding his arms.

'Of course, Chiara, our parents' favorite, would know what was happening in my life even before I do.'

He looked down his nose at her petite frame, easily a foot taller than she and felt his blood boiling.

"What do you know that I don't?" he bristled.

Chiara pressed a hand to her heart.

"Don't tell me you don't know?" she chimed. "Why I thought it was public knowledge by now... You will be replacing Nushka as Ruler of The Pitts of Moor." Her eyes glittering, she waited for his reaction.

Thorn stood frozen. His heart was a thundering beast within him, his palms starting to perspire. He didn't realize when he was sent to interrogate Agnes earlier that it was his only chance to save himself from Nushka's fate. Archè and Aria would banish him for failing to come up with a reason to keep Nushka contained.

If tonight's rebellion did not go to plan, he would be banished to Rule over Moor for all eternity. He would be sent to a place unworthy of even the foulest creatures of the mortal world. He was going to be sick...

Breathing rapid, Thorn attempted to compose himself. Judging by the way Chiara grinned, he knew she had been satisfied by his shocked reaction, though a tinge of disappointment also gleamed in her eyes, likely hoping for him to explode and cause a scene. If Thorn had any regrets about siding with Nushka and Lilith, that guilt was completely eradicated. He was overcome with all-consuming rage. He didn't know why he had expected anything less from the Rulers. Even after knowing all that Lilith and Nushka had endured, some small part of him still thought that Aria and Archè loved their children. How wrong he had been. He and his siblings were merely pawns for the King and Queen to wield as they saw fit. They didn't give a damn about their children's wellbeing.

"Shall we return to the party?" Chiara asked sweetly, but to Thorn her words dripped with poison. "The musicians have finished playing. It seems I have missed all the fun. However, it is time for the King and Queen to begin the ceremony, so you'd best end whatever was going on out here and join us inside," she prodded.

Thorn took a deep breath and rolled his shoulders to work out the building tension.

"Very well, sister," he gritted out, taking her arm in his own and leading her into the hall, leaving Agnes to trail behind.

He would not let his anger get the better of him. He had a coup to help his sisters win. And so, the God of War began descending into his power, and whenever Lilith and Nushka made their move, he decided he would join them too.

The banquet hall had quieted when Thorn and Chiara re-entered through one of the arched doorways. Upon the dais on the opposite side of the room, Archè and Aria held court from their thrones. The room filled with Deities and magical creatures hung on their every word as they praised Nushka, who stood beside their thrones. Lilith stood on her other side, her eyes strangely vacant.

"...and so," Archè continued, chest puffed with a sense of self-importance, "we welcome our daughter, Nushka, back to the Land of the Gods. Here, we are sure she will flourish and blossom in her new role, just as I am sure her replacement will thrive ruling over The Pitts of Moor. Ruling over Moor is a vital peacekeeping role that helps maintain the barriers between good and evil. We thank Nushka for her many eons of service in that position," he announced, his speech oozing condescension.

Nushka thanked the King of the Gods for his *generous* words, and the Ruler of the Gods raised his glass in answer.

'Now is my chance to tell my sisters I have their backs.'

"Excuse me, Your Majesty," Thorn bellowed from the other side of the room, dropping Chiara's arm and pushing through the crowd. "I have something I wish to say."

Thorn felt like an unwanted guest interrupting a wedding ceremony, but he pushed on. He had to show his sisters he was on their side before it was too late. He needed them to see that he cared. Fury burned in Archè's gaze at the disruption, his fists clenched at his sides, but for the sake of maintaining appearances, he pasted a smile across his face.

"Very well, my son. Make your way to the dais and tell us all how proud you are of your sister and how you can't wait to take her place." His words were a double-edged sword, his shoulders tightening in warning.

The crowd parted for Thorn as he strode the last few feet to the dais and ascended the stairs. Archè resumed his seat atop the throne and beckoned with a flourish of his hand for Thorn to continue. Nushka titled her head at him but he ignored her unspoken question and instead addressed the audience who waited eagerly to hear what he had to say.

Thorn inhaled deeply.

"I would like to first thank my father for appointing me as the new Ruler of Moor," he declared.

The audience began whispering amongst themselves excitedly. His *promotion,* as Chiara had put it, was clearly hot gossip. He paused his speech until the room had quieted once more.

"As I was saying, I could not imagine taking on a more important role. Being the God of War myself, it feels like I was born for the position." He chuckled jovially through his teeth. "Who wouldn't want to be banished to such an uninhabitable realm for all eternity?" he added with a grin that didn't reach his eyes. It had the desired effect. The audience gasped, the patrons stilling.

Archè lurched from his seat. "I think you have said enough," the King of the Gods sneered. "Let us return to our celebration."

"I couldn't agree more, Your Highness," he agreed, before turning to Lilith and Nushka and offering an exaggerated bow.

"If you are ever in need of my assistance, I will always be there to support you," Thorn promised before snatching Nushka's wine glass and holding it up for the room to see.

"To Nushka!" he enthusiastically toasted. "May the Land of the Gods welcome her with open arms, just as they have done so for me!"

Thorn pretended to drink deeply from the goblet, but not a drop passed his lips. Before him, the room of Deities, magical creatures, and servants, awkwardly toasted and drank with him, including, to his relief, the King and Queen of the Gods. And just like that, it was done.

Whatever Nushka and Lilith had planned, the next move was up to them. He silently prayed that his sisters saw his offer for what it was; an alliance and a heartfelt promise disguised as a toast. He would help make the bastard Rulers pay for all they had done.

War was coming... and he was ready for it.

The Goddess of Blood and Bone

Atop the dais, the Goddess of Blood and Bone saw her chance and seized it. Nushka's powerful dark blood—the very same that ran diluted through Hyacinth—was capable of great things, including activating the potion on the High Witch's behalf. A potion that now weaved its way into the stomachs of every Deity in the banquet hall bar Lilith, Thorn and herself. The God of War's cooperation had been a fortunate surprise; one she could not afford to sneer at. She would ponder his motives later, but for now, she needed every ally she could gather.

Nushka raised her arms ceremoniously above her head. Dark shadow magic began billowing throughout the room, urging the potion slumbering within the bellies of her enemies to nullify their powers and drain their strength. The room became a cacophony of sound once more as confused, frightened, or furious Deities watched the scene unravel before them. Someone in the room triggered an alarm as the audience—who were temporarily blinded by her dark shadow magic—called out for help from guards that were nowhere to be found.

The Goddess of Blood and Bone, in a deep voice not wholly of this world, began chanting the spell Hyacinth, the High Witch of the wendigast, had composed for her:

"Schediáste ti dýnamí sas, párte ti dýnamí sas.
Draw thy strength, take thy power.
Schediáste ti dýnamí sas, párte ti dýnamí sas.
Draw thy strength, take thy power.
Schediáste ti dýnamí sas, párte ti dýnamí sas.
Draw thy strength, take thy power."

Nushka recited the spell over and over, entwining her dark magic around the words she spoke, sensing the rising magic stirring within the Deities in the room. Ancient words to activate the eons-old enchantment that Hyacinth had installed within the potion curling through the veins of each of her foes. A variation of the potion that Hyacinth had used upon her own clan many centuries ago in a forest full of wendigast, who had danced daringly around bonfires beneath a full moon.

As the Goddess of Blood and Bone's chanting built, dark shadows billowed from the King of the Gods who launched his power upon Nushka, assaulting her with his own dark magic. The essence of the ether lashed at her in the form of shadow whips. Distracted by the lashings she fended off with her own powers, she did not notice the King's shadows creeping along the floor subtly edging their way towards her.

Nushka's power stuttered as she choked and gagged on snakes of dark wind that climbed her body and funnelled into her mouth, drawing the air from her lungs. Her vision blurred as the oxygen and life was drained from her. Archè sent a cyclone of wind pummelling into her side knocking her to the ground.

A torrent of dark wind lashed at her from all sides like sharp knives. All the while the essence of darkness sucked the air from her lungs. Nushka panicked, her body thrashing about at the King's endless assault. Drawing upon the dark power she had been funnelling from deep within over the previous days, her magic exploded in wave of blessed relief, pushing the Kings shadows back. The pressure that had swelled within her eased at the expulsion of so much power.

A shield of shadow wind snapped into place around her after the last of the King's power was expelled from her lungs. Hunched on her hands and knees Nushka gasped for breath. Her vision slowly cleared.

Panting, Nushka resumed her chants as she sluggishly pulled herself to her feet. Wounds peppering her body caused her to hiss as she rose. She had to diffuse the King's powers or else all would be lost. The King lashed at her shield with everything he had. He did not hold back. With each fresh assault of the King's power the barrier shuddered and weakened. It would not hold out for long against Archè's full strength. The King of the Gods lashed at her with all he had, trying desperately to break through the shield and bring the Goddess down. He would do whatever it took to destroy her and keep his crown.

Drawing up another well of power, The Goddess of Darkness retaliated, thrusting a fierce wave of infernal power at the King. Her aim was perfect and the effect of her strike was devastating. Archè pummelled into a nearby column before slumping to the ground. The King shuddered in pain, his eyes flaring widely as his powers began to finally dissipate.

'Thank the stars,' Nushka thought as she chanted more fiercely now, eager to bring down the King.

With the last dregs of Archè's power, he opened a portal beside him leading to a pocket realm where his guards were gathered, ready to protect and serve.

Nushka had wondered where he had kept the winged warrior legion all this time; had wondered why she had not seen any of the guards in attendance during their short stay. It seemed her father had a contingency plan in place. Unfortunately, she would had expected nothing less from the King.

With her protective shield of shadow magic wrapped securely around her, and the chant now finally complete, Nushka lowered her arms. She grinned, sharp teeth gleaming in feral delight, her hair a writhing beast behind her. One by one she beheld each Deities' light dimming from within, their auras flicking out like candles, until they appeared wholly mortal, sapped of their giftings and power. Many had grown cocky over the years, deeming combat lessons beneath them, becoming completely reliant on their powers. It was those same immortals that now stood dumbfounded and completely defenceless.

For the first time in her awfully long existence, Nushka beheld shock in the King and Queen's faces as they too were rendered completely powerless. Aria's usually radiant aura of light was completely muted as she cowered behind her throne.

Streams of pterocentaur, with the torso and upper bodies of an immortal and the lower body and wings of a pegasus, cantered through Archè's portal, wings tucked in tight, their weapons poised and ready to attack. With an eruption of power, Nushka opened an immense portal between her and the approaching winged warriors, unleashing all manner of wicked creatures upon the hall. It was time for her dark army to make their grand entrance.

Deities were launched into the air, bound by vines that miraculously descended from the ceiling at the wendigast witches' commands. Hyacinth herself led the charge, clad in leather armour that she so rarely wore. Stunned Gods and Goddesses alike were bound with tree roots that emerged at the High Witch's summons, snaring their limbs and pegging them forcefully to the ground.

Deities close enough to the staircase at the far end of the hall fled, heading for the lower levels, eager to escape the coming bloodshed. Thorn, much to Nushka's fury, helped them escape, erecting a shield of impenetrable wind to protect the backs of those who made their dash for freedom.

The pterocentaur legion shot the wendigast warriors with fire-tipped arrows. Some missed, but many found their marks in the bark plated clothes, felling many of the witch tree spirits in a single hit; their bodies erupting into flames. Lilith raced across the hall, sending her shadow magic spearing for the King's warriors—not to eliminate them, much to Nushka's disgust—but simply to incapacitate them. It seemed Ilbis had not been exhaustive enough with his gifting when he had altered her sister's thoughts. Had he been fully successful in his task, Lilith would have not only forgotten about what had taken place in The Pitts of Moor, but also followed the order to abandon her empathetic nature and develop the same bloodlust that dwelled within Nushka. Regardless, she was a formidable asset to Nushka's cause, defending her Dark Army ruthlessly with her incredible shadow gifting.

A rogue winged centaur broke away from the herd and attempted to dodge between the ensnared Deities, weaving his way towards the dais, only to be met with Ilbis himself as he entered through the portal. Ilbis's eyes flared, and the soldier stilled, entrapped in his gaze. The guard's vision glazed over, his jaw slackening as Ilbis used his telepathic gifting upon the male, manipulating his mind and taking away his free will. Several heartbeats later, the warrior's gaze hardened and his nostrils flared. Released of Ilbis's mental grasp, he turned and galloped back to his own herd and unleashed himself upon his fellow legionnaires. Steel on steel clashed as the guard was forced to battle his own kind. He felled nine of his fellow pterocentaurs before a sword pierced his heart and he fell to the ground, never to rise again.

The cruelty of the battle delighted Nushka as she fed upon the fear and violence emanating in the room, replenishing her strength, her outstretched claws eager to shred flesh and draw blood. Nushka's shadow power raged, reaching out from her, seeking out her prey and attacking without mercy.

Ilbis, dressed in ancient armour infused with bone, was thrilled to unleash himself upon the Deities and pterocentaur. The ground trembled beneath his heavy steps, an aura of power radiating from him. With his mind control gifting and combat skills with a sword, he was a force to be reckoned with, manipulating multiple Gods and legionnaires at a time into turning upon each other. Stripped of all control over their minds, Nushka watched as friends and family ripped each other apart into blood ribbons.

Ilbis's soulless children, the ghouls, descended upon the trapped and injured Deities like hordes of hungry monsters, feeding off their life's essence. The Goddess of Blood and Bone relished in her enemies suffering as they walked a fine line between life and death. She marvelled at the blood bath drenching the hall, the smell of copper in the air. Only hours earlier, these same Deities had danced, entranced by lust.

Pterocentaur and vengeful Deity alike, with unhealthy disregard for their own safety, took turns launching themselves at Nushka armed only with their weapons. Arrows aimed with skilled precision turned to ash as they met her shield of dark wind. Her wicked shadows, near sentient, now invigorated with renewed strength, lashed and sunk their claws into approaching prey revelling in the pain it caused.

As winged warriors perished, more entered the fray through the King's portal replacing their numbers. They fought fearlessly with sword, dagger, bow and arrow, motivated by their foolish courage to protect the entrapped Deities from further harm. Others formed a barricade near the staircase, in the hopes of preventing Nushka's dark army from descending the stairs and attacking the now powerless immortals that had managed to flee the carnage.

Nearby, one of the wendigast witches was attacked by a pterocentaur as she tried to retrieve a potion from her belt. She released an ear-piercing shriek as his sword impaled in her lower abdomen sending her thumping to the ground and the light fading from her eyes. One of her clan members bellowed in anger as she summonsed a vine from the ground that wrapped around the warrior's four legs, trapping him where he stood. As he slashed with his spare sword at the vines, more ascended replacing the binds quicker than he could sever them. Out of reach of the witch, without a bow or other weapon to defend himself, the wendigast hurled a glass vial at the guard that shattered against his side and froze him in place. Fire burned in the witch's woodland eyes as she beheld her fallen sister's body.

The warrior wrapped her gangly hands awkwardly around the hilt of the impaled sword and removed the weapon from her sister abdomen with one strong pull. The wendigast's lip curled back revealing jagged fangs as she stalked toward the guard, her spider silk hair trailing behind her. With a surge of adrenaline running through her veins, spurred on by her need for revenge, the witch decapitated her enemy with one sweep of his own sword. With a flare of her elemental wind magic, she sent the frozen guard crashing to the ground.

Mandigon led the edimmu next, following the last of Ilbis's ghouls. Their species fed upon the life forces of the newly injured that the ghouls missed, as they weaved their way through the room, sparing none in their wake.

Peuchen slithered out of the portal that had expanded in size to accommodate their larger bodies and wingspans. Towering over every being in the room, they made their way towards the balconies and launched themselves into the moonlit sky. As planned, they were to attack anyone who fled the castle. As the serpent dragons made their way to the balconies, their enemies were either trampled or squeezed to death, so tightly that their eyes bulged before their carcasses hit the ground with a thud. Peuchen fed on them eagerly, their sharp fangs dripping red.

The chimera herd led by Zeri, entered the hall, bringing up the rear of the Goddess's dark army. The portal back to The Pitts dissipated into shadow behind them. The vicious beasts pounced over the entrapped Deities still bound by the remaining witches' magical vines coming to the wendigast witches' aid.

Zeri began bounding eagerly to their master's side, which drew a small smile to Nushka's lips. But, instead of praising Zeri for its loyalty, she commanded her pet return to the fray to fight. The last of the pterocentaurs numbers having finally entered the hall, the portal to the other realm dematerialised. Zeri huffed their annoyance, tail flicking in irritation at the dismissal. Reluctantly, the bhoot turned its four paws around and re-joined the herd, tearing through pterocentaur wings and limbs with each of its three heads.

Pride swelled within the Goddess of Blood and Bone's shrivelled heart as she watched her loyal pet tear through her enemies, rallying to her cause. She made a mental note to gift the pet with a few of her enemies' fleshy bones to gnaw on when the fighting was over.

Around the Goddess, to her fascination and utter pleasure, she noticed the felled bodies extended in all directions in a radius of at least twenty feet away. The bodies of her enemies oozed dark blood from every orifice. The pupils of their sightless eyes lay open permanently, dilated in fear. Her dark shadows had been busy, it seemed.

The Goddess gazed at the carnage taking place. Barely a dent had been made in her army's numbers, with the unfortunate exception of the wendigast. The fighting had now spread out to the surrounding balconies and the sky beyond, their numbers too great to squeeze within the hall.

Nushka looked back to where she had last remembered seeing the Rulers of the Gods cowering behind a column, but they were gone. How long had it been since she had seen them? Or Agnes, for that matter? Not that her handmaiden's whereabouts mattered all that much. The brat had likely fled the room with the Deities at the beginning of the battle like a spineless coward. But the King and Queen... She needed to find them and hold them accountable for their actions. The Goddess of Blood and Bone had a debt to settle.

☽ 25 ☾

Agnes

One moment Agnes was following Thorn and Chiara into the banquet hall, and the next was utter chaos. The plan to imbue the Deities with the tainted wine had gone off without a hitch. Everyone who had tasted the nectar had quickly found themselves powerless after Nushka activated the potion.

As soon as the handmaiden had heard the Goddess of Blood and Bone's chants, she began making her way towards the exit. Agnes was not one to fear or turn away from facing the consequences of her actions, but she maintained a healthy level of desire for self-preservation.

Then it happened. The first strike upon the Rulers.

Thanks to a direct assault to the chest with Nushka's shadow magic, Archè slammed against a column beside Agnes. The King of the Gods roared in pain, making furious eye contact with Agnes as he slumped to the ground. Before he could order her to be seized, Agnes burst into an all-out sprint for the stairs. She had planned her escape in the dark dungeon cell of Moor, had memorized the layout of the castle in the sky for this very moment. Right now, she couldn't have been more grateful for her brief time in possession of the Orb of Historia.

Several Deities looked upon her quizzically as she weaved hastily between them, heading for the exit. One God tried to seize her by her red silk gown, but only air raked his fingers as Agnes lunged to the side just in time to escape his grasp.

A blazing crack of thunder sounded, and a radiating light illuminated the hall as Archè opened a portal beside where he lay. Agnes couldn't help herself as she paused briefly to turn around and re-assess the situation.

Creating the portal had been the King of the God's dramatic final stand. The God's powers were completely drained now. The Deities, whose powerful, light-filled auras previously radiated from them, were now dimmed, making them appear strangely human. Many looked around in disbelief, unable to comprehend such a loss. Others clung to their chests as if their souls had been torn away, and they were incapable of living without that spark of power. Others were furious—rightly so—begging their loved ones to flee as they turned to face the threats of the Goddess of Darkness and the Goddess of Blood and Bone.

Past the gaping, wide-eyed Deities, through the portal, began streaming a seemingly endless line of the King's guards: the pterocentaurs.

'I have to get out of here now!'

One of the winged guards briefly peered in her direction, but now hidden amongst the muted Deities, Agnes no longer stood out from the crowd or drew their attention. His gaze soon moved on, and he too began approaching the dais like the rest of his herd.

A second portal, one of darkness and intolerable heat, opened into the banquet hall. Smoke billowed as Nushka's army made their terrifying grand entrance, unleashing nightmares upon the unsuspecting Deities. Agnes watched on as Nushka's wicked army met the pterocentaur guard.

The violence and mayhem that ensued rivaled what she had witnessed in The Pitts, except this time it was the innocent that would pay the price. Immortals rendered powerless and incapable of defending themselves, were about to be caught in the middle of a battle that many would not walk away from. Their only crime had been following Rulers who only cared for the elite.

Agnes resumed her sprint, only a dozen strides separating her from the staircase that would lead her to safety. She desperately needed somewhere to hide and wait out the rest of the devastating battle. After Nushka, Lilith, and their dark army had defeated the enemy, she would return and face the mess that she had helped create.

Agnes neared the top of the staircase just as vines ascended out of the ground and dropped from the ceiling in search of victims to ensnare, thanks to the powerful wendigast that descended upon the hall. Screams of agony ripped from the throats of ally and foe alike.

Regardless of how well Nushka had planned the attack, there would always be casualties on both sides. Agnes pitied the witches who met their ends at the hands of the pterocentaur, just as she found herself pitying the immortals caught up in the fight.

Agnes watched as a wendigast who was using her magic to heal a fellow injured witch, was shot with a flaming arrow that embedded in her chest through the plated bark gown. Her traditional garb erupted in a whir of fire and smoke. Agnes would never forget her piercing scream as the arrow met its mark, nor the way she continued shrieking as she burned to death.

Agnes hurled her stomach's contents on the floor.

The long-lived witch's end had been unnecessary. Even if Agnes hadn't wielded the bow that shot the witch, she still felt as though she had played a role in bringing about her demise. She tried to rationalize to herself that a war would have occurred whether she helped drug the Deities or not. But it was no use. As she beheld creatures and immortals alike on both sides meeting their deaths, she couldn't help but feel partially responsible.

From the top of the staircase, Thorn stood guard, protecting all those that pushed past one another, ready to use their neighbor as a shield to ensure their own safety. The battle brought out the worst in the immortals. His magic whipped an impenetrable barrier of protection around those who drew within several stride lengths of the staircase. Sweat slid down Thorn's brow at the effort of maintaining the protective shield.

She ran to him. "Thorn, we need to get out of here," she begged him.

He seized her by the arm and drew her near. "Where do you think you're going!" he growled, fury and contempt coating his every word.

"To find somewhere safe to hide," Agnes winced, pulling her arm free of his grasp.

Thorn sneered at her in revulsion.

"Typical!" he spat. "You were so quick to bring The Pitts down upon my people, but the moment your existence is at risk, you run and hide like a coward!"

"I know I'm a coward," she cried, tears welling in her eyes. "I am the worst kind of soul there is. This is all my fault and I want to run away, but I don't know what else to do. I don't know how to make this better! I can't stop this!"

Her body trembled, as anxiety consumed her.

A pterocentaur slammed into one of Thorn's wind barriers before falling lifeless to the floor, blood trickling from his nose. Cold, sightless eyes stared up towards the ceiling. Agnes flinched at the sight. The God of War stood there, beads of sweat trickling down his brow, muscled arms taut and his hands once more outstretched before him. The effort of maintaining the shields was taking all his focus and energy.

"These are my people," he managed to say through gritted teeth. "Hating my parents and supporting my sisters does not mean I will stand by and watch innocents be murdered. I will have no part in that!"

Agnes paused for a moment. He really was a good God, she realized. Thorn wanted to help his sisters, but he also couldn't tolerate seeing defenseless people getting hurt. She felt unworthy of him. Guilt would haunt her after today, she knew that, and she knew that she deserved it. She felt like worthless trash. No matter how much she wanted to change her life, death and destruction would always follow her.

"I'm sorry Thorn. I'm sorry for all of it," she vowed.

Thorn turned back to her, each movement a struggle as he focused his efforts on protecting the retreating Deities.

"I know," he rasped. "And it's not all your fault. I'm as much to blame for this as you."

Agnes's eyes widened. Thorn flinched, his mouth grimacing, brow furrowed in concentration.

"I... I care about you," he promised.

Agnes didn't know what to say, her breathing hitched. She wrapped her arms around him even as his arms were outstretched, even as he shook from the strain of overexerting his powers.

"And I for you..." she murmured. "Thank you for not giving up on me."

The words out of her mouth sounded hollow, inadequate. But there were no other words to convey how grateful she was that he understood her, cared for her, and didn't condemn her as she deserved.

"Go." He begged her in between heaving breaths. "Go hide. Then come back after all this is over and together, we'll fix this mess."

"I will," she promised, "I mean it."

Agnes stood on her toes and pressed a kiss to his cheek.

"Don't die on me!" she jeered him breaking the tension. He huffed a laugh but kept his focus on the task at hand.

She pushed down the feeling of guilt that would only hold her back now. What was done was done. She would ruminate on her failings later. For now, she needed to get to safety so she could exist long enough to make up for all the pain she had caused. She descended the stairs and did not look back.

Hiding was no longer an option. The castle had gone into lockdown, chaos spreading far and wide. Wherever Agnes ventured, hordes of terrified Deities had already sought shelter, so she embarked upon her next best option.

It had taken Agnes longer than expected to reach the stables on the lower levels of the castle in the sky. Unfortunately, she was not the only one who had considered such an escape plan. Powerless Deities fought to untether the pegasi from their stalls. The mighty winged horses were twice the size of regular horses, their coats a variety of neutral colors. Their feathered wings tucked in protectively by their sides, as they arched to get away from the Gods and Goddesses that brawled for their reins. The fighting, both in the stables and in the levels above, startled many of the mythical beasts, causing them to rear. One of the stable hands had been trampled beneath a particularly skittish ebony beast and the Gods now gave it a wide birth.

Agnes had grown up around horses. Her Royal family owned a large stable with an array of prized stallions and mares. Agnes had been riding since she was a toddler, and so she had developed significant skills in riding, having cared for them during her human life. If anyone could tame the jittery mount, it would be her.

Many levels above, the battle grew louder. Screams pierced the air, and the castle shook as the two armies battled. The sound and vibration further incited panic in pegasus and Deity alike. Deities began jumping on any pegasus they could reach, stating their claim and hastily pulling their children and families onto the saddle in front of them. Fists were thrown and kicks landed as the immortals fought over the mighty winged beasts.

Agnes slowly edged her way around the stall of the dark skittish creature. No one dared follow her, no matter how desperate they were to escape the war zone. The stallion fiercely pulled at its tethered reins, desperate to escape the chaos. The deceased body beneath it was pummeled further into the ground with each stomp of its hooves, turning the flesh into bloody ribbons.

As Agnes edged her way into the creature's line of sight, she raised her arms to placate the beast, making soothing sounds. The pegasus looked at her defiantly, but it soon ceased its stomping, though it continued whinnying, head thrashing against the tether that kept it contained. Agnes knew better than to untie a wild horse until it had fully calmed. There was a good chance that she would end up being his next stall mat if she did. But she needed to earn the beast's trust quickly, fearful that Archè's guards were searching for her. Laying low was not an option; chaos had descended too quickly and spread too far. There was nowhere safe to hide anymore.

Without over-analyzing it, and before she lost her nerve, Agnes reached for the pole at the far end of the stall and untied the stallion's tether. The creature's reins fell free.

The pegasus stilled before turning to her, eyes wide with rage, nostrils flaring. Its gaze burned through to her very soul and, whatever it beheld, the creature did not shy form. Perhaps it found a kindred spirit in Agnes. An angry, hate-filled, fearless beast seeking freedom, much like the handmaiden before him.

Agnes bowed before the mythical creature and the pegasus huffed in recognition, lowering its head in permission for Agnes to climb upon its back. Ever so slowly, giving the pegasus a chance to reconsider, Agnes grabbed the nearby step ladder and approached the mount's side. Slowly and gently, she grabbed the reins and threaded them over the creature's bowed head. After positioning and ascending the step ladder, she grabbed the horn of the saddle and slid her left foot into the stirrup. She didn't give herself a chance to reconsider as she heaved herself up and over the horse's back. With the gate already open behind them, the pegasus stormed for the exit and into the chaos of the stables.

A loud bray of warning ripped from the winged beast's maw and the Deities blocking its escape quickly dove out of the way. Those already atop a pegasus urged their beasts onwards to the exit ramp.

One by one, the pegasi galloped with all their might down the ramps and launched themselves into the open air, engaging their wings and flying away. Agnes's mount grew tired of waiting and he pushed his way to the front of the queue. Sheer power had the pegasus roaring down the take-off ramp, faster and steadier than all before him. As he unfurled his ebony wings, catching an updraft, they launched into the air and Agnes's heart plummeted into her stomach.

Clouds billowed around them as the beast's mighty wings flapped either side of Agnes, soaring fearlessly through the night sky. Its ebony coat blended with its surroundings. She held onto the reins as if her very existence depended on it, digging her knees into the creature's sides, trying desperately to remain in the saddle. All around them pegasi and riders fled the castle in the sky in search of safety. Then the peuchen arrived.

The peuchen had arrived on massive, deep-purple dragon wings, and they were itching for blood. The peuchen were a fearsome force in the Dark Goddess's army, and right now their sights were set on the herd of pegasi and the riders trying to make their escape.

The peuchen dwarfed even the pegasi. Their massive serpent-like bodies were akin to their basilisk cousins, defying gravity as their enormous, scaled wings carried them through the air. Their sharp fangs and forked tongues promised pain and death.

It was then that Agnes realized the risks of flying amongst a herd of their enemy. Only now, as they attempted to flee the onslaught of the peuchen, did she really consider how thoroughly fucked she was now that the Deities looked like mere humans. To the peuchen, she was just another Goddess about to meet her end.

"Oh, fuck! Dive, boy, dive!" Agnes coaxed the beast beneath her, urging him on with a hard kick of her heels, lashing at his reins.

The mighty pegasus needed no encouragement. The wild-hearted beast sharply dove away from the pegasus herd, trying desperately to lose the peuchen now swarming towards them. As they zigzagged through the cloudy night sky, Agnes struggled to see their surroundings. The darkness made the escape even more treacherous; a fact which terrified Agnes. Thoughts of blindly crashing into another mythical beast, or worse, possibly colliding into a mountain or the ground far below came to the forefront of her mind.

Higher up, flashes of fire billowed from the peuchens' maws, the charred or severed remains of pegasus and rider alike dropping like unholy rain around them. Agnes's mount dodged the falling remnants with liquid grace, so different from the skittish beast she had met in the stables. In the skies, he was king.

Down and down, they descended, her mount pushing itself to its very limits to create as much distance as possible between them and the peuchen. High above, the serpent dragons pursued their prey with such deadly efficiency, none stood a chance against them. Agnes's heart plummeted in her chest at the speed and degree at which they made their descent, uncertain how she had not already fallen out of the saddle and to her doom.

Searing agony fired through her as an arrow embedded in her chest. Agnes's eyes flared in sudden shock as she screamed, the pain so overwhelming she dropped the pegasus's reins and slipped off her fierce mount's back. The wind clawed at her face, blinding her as she plummeted towards a sandstone structure. It all happened so fast her mount did not have time to react before he too was shot from the sky with another arrow.

She knew the fall would not kill her, knew the arrow could not kill her. But the pain of her bones shattering into a million pieces once she landed would make the ache in her chest pale in comparison. Her vision blurred as she continued to fall until mighty hands of a creature caught her in its strong, muscular arms.

Agnes heaved a shallow sigh of relief. Thorn had come for her. Despite everything, he had come for her. He did care for her. Her heart fluttered, and all she wanted to do was lose herself in his touch.

She looked up, wanting to peer into his eyes and kiss him. But instead of the familiar brown gaze of the God of War, cold, green eyes stared back at her. Then she noticed the steely look upon his face, took in the wings, the bow and quiver hung across his back. A pterocentaur, had captured her. There was nowhere to hide anymore. She had run out of luck. She was now in the hands of the enemy.

Searing pain ripped through her chest with every jostle and flap of the pterocentaur's wings. He did not speak to her as they flew back to the castle, but his eyes pierced her with unadulterated hatred and disgust.

Ascending through the clouds, her captor's white wings, bare torso, and light-grey haired lower centaur body blended in flawlessly with the clouds. It was likely how her enemy had remained hidden from them as he hunted them down.

'The poor pegasus. He did not deserve such an end.'

Tears welled in her eyes at the thought of the fierce, wild-hearted beast that met its end defending her. He had tried so desperately to fly them both to safety. Her kindred, strong-willed spirit who would never fly fearlessly again. Without Agnes to garner her enemy's attention, he might have managed to escape. That thought sent guilt pooling in her stomach. She mentally added it to the list of all the things she needed to make amends for.

Agnes winced as another sharp stab of pain jarred through her as the pterocentaur banked a hard right. The King's guard flared his wings to lower their speed, then glided silently onto one of the lower-level balconies of the castle.

They were not alone.

The pterocentaur guard dropped Agnes unceremoniously on the hard sandstone floor. Screaming from the impact, Agnes nearly fainted from the surge of agony as the arrow in her chest impaled further, breaking clean through her back. Stars flashed and her vision dotted as she gasped, tears tracking down her cheeks.

Had she not garnered the Goddess of Blood and Bone's favor five years ago, she would have been subjected to an eternity of torment. Yet here she was in blinding agony, helpless, powerless. If the King commanded it, her fate would be worse than death. Agnes could not imagine such torturous agony for all eternity. She would give anything, do anything, for the pain to end. She wished desperately that Thorn would somehow find her and save her. He was the only one who would care if she were gone.

Agnes was done with all the games. She was sick of enduring. She wanted the pain and all of it to end. She didn't care about her own life. As long as Thorn was safe it was all that mattered. She just wanted to close her eyes and never wake to another horrifying day.

With one steel-capped hoof, the winged guard kicked Agnes where she lay, flipping her over onto her back. She grunted as another wave of intolerable pain coursed through her body. Without warning, he grasped the shaft of the arrow, gave it a decent twist to entice even greater pain within her, and then yanked it out with one fierce pull.

Agnes screamed, her voice now hoarse, blood pooling from the wound in waves. In the absence of the arrow, a gaping hole in her chest remained. She had never wanted to be in spirit form so much as this moment. Agnes drew blood as she bit down hard on her lip, not wanting to give the guard the satisfaction of hearing her suffer anymore. She would not appear weak before those who wished her harm. She may have reached the limit; it was true she would welcome oblivion, but she would not give her captors the satisfaction of seeing her squirm anymore.

"Bring her here," an ancient voice spat from within the confines of the room.

Fear and dread overcame her. Agnes knew that voice, knew that rich accent all too well. The voice that was so much like his son's. A pang of heartache ripped through her chest at the thought of the God who was nothing like his sadistic father.

The pterocentaur grasped Agnes by the hair and yanked her across the hard floor through the balcony entrance. The guard's hand, fisted amongst her blonde hair, tore hair from her scalp as he tugged her further into the room, discarding her at the foot of her enemy.

'Holy rutting Gods.'

"You," Archè growled.

All false pretense was abandoned as the true face of the King of the Gods stared down at Agnes. The same Deity who banished each of his children to different realms, so they could not challenge his seat of power. Before Agnes was a male who would do anything to save himself.

"Me," Agnes droned in return, quirking an eyebrow.
She had nothing left to give but this one ounce of defiance. Her body ached, her wound was agonizing. Had she been human, she was sure vital organs would have been ruptured and she'd be dead long ago. Unfortunately, whatever miracle had prevented her from feeling pain upon her arrival had died off along with the Deities' powers. Perhaps it had been the Gods and not the realm that had

prevented her from such discomfort. It explained how Thorn had been able to harm her during her interrogation...

Quivering, battered and bruised and shielded behind her husband, was Aria. Beneath the firelight of the single lit candle, the Queen of the Gods was a mere shadow of the female she had been earlier that day. Agnes could not help the smirk that drew upon her lips at the sight of how far the pair had fallen. Even though she felt remorse for the role she had played in the countless innocent lives lost today, she was still glad to see their Rule come to an end. She had helped to bring down an entire dynasty, and now she would pay dearly for it, just like she deserved. She only prayed to the universe that Archè lost his temper and destroyed her quickly.

A noise sounded at the door, drawing the room's attention. Someone, or something, rattled the handle, trying to break the lock. Thumping sounded and the door shook as the mystery intruder tried to break into the room.

Archè launched for Agnes, grabbing her by the scruff of the neck to hold a blade to her throat. The blade would not kill her, but it would hurt, and it would convey his message clearly enough.

Perhaps decapitating her in this form *could* result in wiping her from eternity. Perhaps not only magic was needed to accomplish the task. For the first time, she had no answer, and despite her resignation that she was ready to depart the afterlife, it scared her.

There was so much more Agnes realized she wanted to accomplish, and there is no better motivator than death. Nothing more clarifying than facing down the blade. A flame awoke inside her, breathing purpose into Agnes despite the agonizing pain coursing through her. There were so many more experiences she wanted to have before she inevitably passed into the ether. She wanted desperately to spend more time with Thorn. She wanted to see what the future beheld for them both, either as a friendship or perhaps something more. Perhaps by some miracle there was the possibility of a better afterlife in store for her.

The pterocentaur guard stepped before his master and captive, prepared to do whatever it took to defend his Rulers at all costs.

'If the stupid fool knew what was good for him, he would abandon his masters and seek refuge in the sky. He will die for his loyalty to these monsters.' Agnes rolled her eyes despite her dire circumstances.

Then the guard drew the bow from his back and notched an arrow into place. Pulling the string back, he took aim at whatever was about to crash through the now splintering door. Aria hid behind her husband, as if she could make herself invisible through sheer willpower.

Finally, the door burst open, its hinges ripped clean off the frames. With a heavy thud it landed on the floor before them and in stalked the Goddess of Blood and Bone, riding Zeri in chimera form. Nushka's shadows writhed with the promise of vengeance.

The Goddess of Blood and Bone grinned in feral delight, claws extended as fluid leaked down the pterocentaur's hind legs. To his credit he did not balk at her presence as he released the arrow from its notch.

Nushka's wicked grin only broadened as she stopped the arrow midair with her dark magic, turning it back on its wielder.

The arrow found its mark in the guard's loyal heart and the mighty winged centaur crumpled to the ground.

He did not rise again.

☽ 26 ☾

The Goddess of Blood and Bone

The battle, if you could even call it that, had been over just as quickly as it had begun.

Above, in the banquet hall bound with vines, the surviving Deities awaited their fate. Hyacinth fortunately remained amongst the living, though many of her coven did not. She was now in charge of over-seeing their captives. The High Witch's gaze was now a little less bright.

Nushka felt a slither of remorse cross her blackened heart for the witches. Their clan had suffered the greatest number of casualties of all the wicked creatures in her army. As hard as the blow would be to Hyacinth, she had known the cost of war, had likely anticipated this very scenario, and yet she had still led her clan into battle. The mighty wendigast race was now on the verge of extinction.

All those who died in service of the Dark Queen would be welcomed into Moor as war heroes. Quarters would be allocated for them in the bone castle, in the same wing as Nushka's favored departed souls. In Moor, they would be free to live out their eternities in whatever depraved manner they saw fit. For many of her followers, that would be enough to placate their remaining living kin. For the wendigast clan, an existence in Moor without access to their former magic would not satisfy.

Nushka had pondered offering the departed wendigast souls the opportunity to ascend to the Afterworld should they wish it, but Hyacinth had objected to the idea. She assured the Goddess of Blood and Bone that her departed coven sisters, who would no longer have anything to fear from the lava plains, would be more comfortable amongst their likeminded kind in The Pitts. It could never replace the freedom and magic they had formerly treasured, but it was a good offer, nonetheless.

Nushka had promised Hyacinth that, unlike many who resided in Moor, the fallen wendigast would never be subjected to pain of any kind. Later she would decree it in writing with her blood; a binding contract in the eyes of the immortals. It was the least Nushka could do to repay them for their service and sacrifice.

The Dark Queen, as a rare gesture of good will, then extended an open invitation to Hyacinth to return to Moor as she saw fit to help her fallen sisters' transition into their new homes. It was the only time she had ever treated her entrusted souls with genuine compassion, and she could tell Hyacinth appreciated the thought, though neither would speak of it. To acknowledge such kindness would be weak, and the two women were anything but.

Astride Zeri, Nushka surveyed the room and its inhabitants with utter revulsion. Two peuchen, at her telepathic summons, landed on the balcony on the other side of the room, sending aftershocks through the floor. They informed their Dark Queen mind-to-mind that the pegasus and their riders had been dealt with. There were no survivors. The Goddess of Blood and

Bone nodded her head in acknowledgement. The ruthlessness of their actions sent a chill of delight down her spine.

'You have done your Dark Queen a great service,' Nushka praised them in return.

All exits were blocked. Not that Archè or Aria stood a chance of escaping. Deprived of his powers, her father sneered at her, dagger pressed to Agnes's chin.

"What in the Afterworld do you think you are doing, Archè?" Nushka asked perplexed, whilst scratching behind her pet's ears. Her sharp claws remained extended in warning.

Archè arrogantly straightened, drawing Agnes closer now, droplets of blood beading at her neck. A large, open wound gaped in her chest.

'Interesting...' she mused.

"What is it that you hope to achieve through this ridiculous display?" she chuckled darkly. "I hold your people captive. Your pterocentaur guards are all dead. No one is coming to rescue you." She smiled wickedly, savoring the bloodlust still coursing through her veins.

Aria tried and failed to make herself even smaller behind her husband. Such a coward. From Ruler of the Gods to powerless immortal. Such a fall. The thought filled Nushka with wicked delight.

Nushka tilted her head, pressing her lips together in thought.

"Once all this is over, I wonder if I should keep you, Mother, as a pet of sorts. Or, perhaps, you would prefer to be my own personal servant? I could even give you the choice if you like.

Pet or servant? Which will it be?" the Goddess of Blood and Bone taunted, a smile twisting upwards, fangs gleaming.

Nushka's writhing hair paused as it, too, contemplated which mode of action would be the most fulfilling.

Archè shoved Agnes roughly, drawing a hiss from lips.

"Let us go or I will chop your wretched lover into a million tiny pieces. I do not need magic for that," Archè spat, pressing the blade further into her neck. A slow stream of blood began to trickle emphasizing his point.

"Lover?" Nushka laughed, sounding perplexed. "Is that what your think she is to me?"

A full belly laugh escaped her, the cruel edge of her humor echoing through the castle. She couldn't remember the last time something so preposterous had made her laugh.

"Oh, you stupid fool. Why would you think she is my lover?! She is a dispensable pawn in my plan. A toy." Nushka's lip curled as Archè's pupils dilated, her amusement making him see red.

"Go on! Do it then!" she urged, clapping with glee, beaming from ear to ear at the prospect of witnessing such wicked savagery. "Don't make me wait. Carry out your threats and butcher the girl! I would love to watch. It will save me the effort of having to reward her for helping. You'll be doing me a favor actually," she admitted, her face darkening, her shadows uncoiling at her feet.

Agnes's eyes widened with fear, the hope in them dimming.

To prove her point, Nushka lowered herself gracefully from atop Zeri's back and stalked toward Agnes. A protective shield of dark shadows formed around her like a second skin. Death would come to any who attempted to penetrate it. Nushka hoped the King would be so bold as to try. It would save her the trouble of getting her hands dirty.

She stopped an arm's length away from where Archè held Agnes hostage. Beads of perspiration dotted his brow. She could almost feel the anger radiating off him—an echo of his power trying to escape its confines from deep within. But her magic and Hyacinth's serum had been too thorough. It would take nothing short of a miracle for someone to unravel the spell and, by then, there would be no one left alive to benefit from it anyway.

A sword of solid obsidian emerged in Nushka's hand, her extended claws wrapping tightly around the hilt. She could end this and pave the way for her new dynasty with one sweep of her sword.

"Stop!" Aria yelled from behind her husband. "You don't have to do this, Nushka." She quivered, rising from the ground to stand beside her husband, putting herself directly in harm's way.

"Lower your weapon, Archè," Aria commanded in a steely tone Nushka didn't recognize.

The Queen of the Gods placed a hand reassuringly on her husband's back. A faint glimmer of pride stirred in Nushka for her mother finally showing some backbone. It was quickly replaced with nausea at the reason why. Archè and Aria's eyes connected, and Nushka wondered if they could somehow still communicate telepathically despite losing their powers.

"Let her go, darling. We need to surrender. There has been too much bloodshed already. If you do this, she will kill you," Aria warned, tears welling in her eyes. "And I love you too much to bear existing without you. I could not endure it."

Disgust crossed Archè's face at the idea of surrender.

"I will never surrender," he spat. Aria's eyes flared alarmingly.

Nushka doubted he had ever surrendered or backed down on anything in his entire existence. The possibility of her parents submitting was not an option the Goddess of Blood and Bone had considered. She was already imaging how she could use her father as a source of entertainment for her wicked subjects. A reward for all their service.

"What a prize you would make... King turned Jester for my beasts," she cackled. "Well, I suppose I could be merciful... How about this: if you surrender, I promise not to kill you both. I will even allow you and your wife to remain together as a sign of my benevolent kindness. That's a surprisingly good deal! What do you say?"

Relief washed over Aria's race and she released the breath she had held. "Thank you Nushka! Thank you! We will do whatever you want. Just please don't harm us!" Aria begged.

The King flinched, his nose crinkling as his face contorted into a sneer of disgust. "Did you not hear me a second ago?! Do not make promises on my behalf," Archè reprimanded his wife.

He turned his attention on Nushka, rage welling within him, veins throbbing in his neck as his face flushed.

"I will never kneel before a whore! You are no daughter of mine. I would rather be abandoned to the ether than kneel to such a wretched beast," Archè roared.

Zeri growled menacingly behind Nushka, loyally defending its master's honor. She knew that her pet would delight in ripping the King to shreds and would feast on his flesh and bones afterwards. All she needed to do was call upon them.

Nushka's lips twisted into a hateful grin, her eyes dark as her blackened heart. She raised her blade reveling in the fear radiating from her parents and handmaiden.

"You won't surrender?" Nushka asked tauntingly. "You'd rather die than show you daughter an ounce of respect?"

Nushka clucked her tongue, shaking her head.

Eager to teach him a lesson, the Goddess lashed at the King with a whip of her shadows, the strike conveniently also hitting Agnes who he still used as a shield. Both hissed in pain. The latter bowed, causing the knife the King held to slice her neck even deeper. A grimace of pain elicited as tears fell freely from her eyes. The Soul looked pitiful and Nushka took great pleasure in her suffering.

Archè paled, his eyes darting to the blocked balcony exit. The peuchen hissed, slithering slowly closer as if readying to attack.

Aria dropped to her knees, clasping her hands together, begging her, "Stop Nushka! You don't have to do this! You can have whatever you want, just please let us go."

Heaving sobs escaped the now hyperventilating Queen as she trembled in undiluted fear. Nushka had never seen her mother beg for anything in her life and to witness her pathetic hysterics was a priceless gift.

"There is nothing you can give me, that I have not already taken for myself. The time for negotiation is over," she replied with deadly calm.

Her shadows, sensing her growing anticipation as she stalked her prey, gathered around her, inhaling and exhaling in waves of dark magic, ready to strike.

Without a second thought, Nushka sent a whip of her dark magic slicing through Archè's arm, unbinding her handmaiden. Mouth gaping, Archè gasped in pain as wide eyed, and Aria screamed in hysterics. Limb and weapon fell to the ground with a clang, blood spraying everywhere.

Heaving sobs escaped the Queen as Archè grasped the gushing stub with his other hand, trying desperately to apply pressure and stem the flow of blood. Each moan of agony that escaped the King's lips electrified Nushka, as his blood continued to gush from the wound despite his efforts to staunch the bleeding. If he didn't see a healer soon, he would bleed out.

"Shall I pull up a chair and allow your painful death to play out naturally? It wouldn't take long I suppose... I could spare a little more time, it would be a sight to behold. . ." she taunted.

Sheer horror flared in the eyes of her parents.

The King and Queen begged for mercy; their hysterics were likely heard from the banquet hall above. Archè would have offered Nushka the sun in that moment if he could have, just to spare his miserable life.

Their pointless cries for forgiveness fell on deaf ears.

Agnes dove out of the way just in time, and in one smooth sweep of the Goddess's razor-sharp sword, blood rained as Archè's head, then body, fell to the ground.

The King of the Gods was dead.

☽ EPILOGUE ☾

The Goddess of Darkness

Battle weary and numb, long after the fighting had ended, Lilith lounged upon her father's former throne, her slender legs dangling over the chair arm. The Goddess of Darkness's shadows oozed off her like the calm after a storm, now their bloodlust was soothed. Her tattered gown was blood-soaked, and with a lazy flick of her wrist she replaced it with her signature sleek, ebony silk gown. She would *never* stoop to wearing pants, regardless of the setting or their practicality.

The remaining living Deities were detained at the far side of the room by the few uninjured wendigast, overseen by Hyacinth and Ilbis. Lilith still did not trust either of them, even after all they had done for Nushka's cause. Ilbis gave Lilith a smug taunting look, which twisted her stomach in disgust.

The peuchen stood like imposing statues, stationed around the balconies in case any captured immortals decided to tempt fate. The trampled bodies coating the floor would likely be enough of a deterrent on their own, even without the presence of the creatures' barbed tails and sharp, poisonous fangs. Lilith was considering asking Nushka to gift her one of the snake dragons as a pet.

The Goddess of Darkness imagined a youngling dragon serpent curled at the foot of her throne of bone would be an imposing sight for any wicked souls entering her domain. She smiled briefly at the thought, then cursed herself for thinking of the Hall of Shadows with more fondness than it deserved.

'It was a cage, nothing more,' Lilith tutted to herself. *'Though I will be keeping my throne regardless of what the future holds. Perhaps the souls encased within will appreciate the change of scenery...'*

The remainder of Nushka's army had returned through a portal opened by Lilith, back to The Pitts where they would rest and make camp. Many of the chimera had pulled the bodies of friend and foe alike back through the portal with them, presumably to feast upon. Any respect Lilith had felt towards the creatures who fought so valiantly by her side was now replaced with disgust.

The Goddess's heart filled with anger, hatred, and now disgust. For a Goddess who had felt extraordinarily little for eons, the rush of emotions over the past couple of days was wholly unsettling to her.

Lilith had killed more of her own people than she dared to recall tonight. The thought did not sit well with her. Her lips curved into a frown.

'I was never fond of the idea of killing my own kin. I had wanted them to pay for what they had done, but I had never wanted them dead. When had that changed?'

The Goddess of Blood and Bone finally deigned to return to the banquet hall, her face alight with feral glee. It was the first time Lilith had seen her sister since the battle had commenced. Lost to bloodlust's song, she had not searched for Thorn or Nushka until the battle was won.

Now her sister swaggered into the hall with Archè's head in one hand, dragging their mother by a leash of shadow magic with the other. Bile burned Lilith's throat, her stomach roiling at the sight of her father's head. Her heart dropped into her stomach as her sister winked, drunk on her victory.

Beside Nushka, the former Queen of the Gods had been stripped to her undergarments, as if the humiliation of being leashed and the grief of losing her husband were not enough. The sight of Nushka, of what was left of her father and mother, was the first nail in Ilbis's mind control coffin.

Potent feelings of anguish battled against feelings of hate, causing fractures in Ilbis's handiwork. With her mind suddenly a little clearer, Lilith fully comprehended the injustice that had been done to her.

Lilith shot to her feet, gazing furiously at Ilbis, who stood smugly looking up at her. Fury bellowed within at how far Nushka had gone to control her. Blood boiling, Lilith's shadows now raged anew.

The Goddess of Blood and Bone declared herself Queen of the Gods that night, without any consideration towards her siblings. With her dark army at her beck and call, who could argue? Left with no other option, Thorn and Lilith fell into line behind their sister.

It had taken weeks for Lilith to break through each of the barriers of mind control Iblis had subjected her to. Little by little, she felt less a clone of her hate-filled sister, and more like herself. Her mental recovery was, in large thanks, due to Thorn, who acted as her moral compass, helping her see sense.

Her kind-hearted brother, who had beheld what Lilith had been transformed into during the battle, had known straight away that something had been done to her. If felt incredibly disconcerting to the Goddess of Darkness to have her gift of judgment so tainted. Lilith's gift was an extension of herself and not being able to rely on its conviction and reassurance made her feel off balance.

In the months since Nushka had seized control of the Land of the Gods and all other realms, mortal and immortal alike, the universe had become a very dark and different place. There was no place for honesty, integrity, or virtue in Nushka's new world. Morals were now distant, unfamiliar ideals. Weaknesses, Nushka had claimed, that held the Gods back from reaching their *full potential*. Whatever that meant. Nushka was all about reaching your full potential... if it aligned with her wishes.

The Goddess of Blood and Bone kept Aria chained to her like a pet, though she was treated with far more cruelty. Lilith had witnessed Nushka treat Zeri with more decency and respect than she paid their mother. Even going as far as serving Aria's meals in a dog bowl on the floor and denying her the use of utensils. Her sister had even made the former Queen relieve herself on the floor in the formal dining room on more than one occasion, denying her the basic rights of toileting or bathing.

It was only when Nushka claimed she could no longer stand her mother's stench that she allowed Aria to bath in stone-cold water. Nushka said she wanted the former Queen to have a taste of what life was like for the lowest of the low. She claimed it would be a humbling experience for her, an opportunity for personal growth. It made Lilith and Thorn sick to their stomachs, though they were powerless to help Aria. They could not risk Nushka's wrath, not with the dark army lying in wait. Even two powerful Gods could not take on an army without aid.

Archè and Aria's loyal followers and the remaining Deities that had survived the battle, including Chiara, were transported to The Pitts of Moor. There, Nushka's followers delighted in subjecting the powerless Gods to all kinds of cruel torment. Ilbis had been placed in charge as temporary warden of The Pitts as a reward for his loyalty.

Lilith vowed she would not allow her kin to spend their eternity trapped there, not if she and Thorn had anything to do with it. Though her fellow Deities deserved punishment for standing aside while the siblings were so sorely mistreated for all these years, they did not deserve the pain and torture that now filled their endless days. Nushka had gone too far.

The only realm that remained mostly untouched by Nushka's wickedness was the Afterworld. Lilith and Thorn convinced their sister to gift them the realm as a reward for their assistance during the battle, and as a show of good faith in their alliance. Apparently Nushka had promised the Afterworld to her handmaiden, of all people, as part of the bargain for her assistance. As soon as Lilith pointed out the absurdity of the notion, Nushka quickly laughed off the thought and said she had never really meant to hold true to her promise anyway. She did however allow Agnes to ascend to the Afterworld and maintain her corporal form at her request. Lilith was eager to see how her reunion with her family played out.

To Lilith's surprise, her brother had formed some sort of a connection to the soul in question, and more often than not she would spend the night in Thorn's chambers. The relationship, perplexed Lilith, but she did not begrudge her brother his happiness.

Given that Thorn had done little to aid in Nushka's cause, the Goddess of Blood and Bone had been reluctant to reward him. So, in namesake, the Afterworld was officially under Lilith's dominion, with Thorn as her assistant of sorts. Thorn still retained his title as God of War, for now... It did not hold the same value as it did before.

Every week Lilith visited the Hall of Shadows and delved out judgements upon the awaiting souls. If she had not agreed to do so, Nushka would have sentenced each soul to Moor regardless of their worth and lived experience. Lilith didn't mind doing it as it allowed her to use her gifting of discernment. It made her feel as though in this new Universe of Nushka's regime, that she could still make a difference.

One night, Lilith and Thorn fled to the Hall of Shadows, shrouding themselves in a soundproof shield for good measure. Only alone would they make their feelings on Nushka's reign crystal clear. Neither had meant for things to go this far. But Lilith, entrapped in Ilbis's mind control had lost all ability to think for herself during the battle, and Thorn, without allies, had been forced to play along or face the same fate as the other immortals. With each passing day of Nushka's rule, their situation became more dire.

"It is up to us to make things right," Thorn stated.

"It is up to us," Lilith agreed, "to fight back."

The End.

A SHIFTER REBORN

A prequel short story of

The Immortal Deities

Nattie Kate Mason

Amongst the great wolf packs of Shadows Peak, the animal shifter hid. A beast of many forms, the shifter raged from town to town, stealing food and inciting fear. It gained joy from such things. The adrenaline rush, like a drug, was a craving that could never be satisfied. The shifter could not recall its parentage. For all they knew, they were the only one of their kind. They could not recall ever meeting another.

Unlike other shapeshifters, the shifter was not human, and it had never taken a human form. Its animalistic instincts were drawn to predatory beasts, and it usually morphed into a superior version of the natural species of which it imitated.

As the hunters moved between the shadows of the mountain pass, they assessed the pack seeking shelter in the mouth of a cave. As they sought out their prey, the shifter tried its best to appear unremarkable amongst the rest of the pack. Not that there was anything ordinary about the giant wolves that lived amongst the dangerous alpine peaks. To the untrained eye, the pack did not stand out, their white or grey coats blending into the mountainous terrain. But for the warriors of Shadows Peak, who knew the passes and the creatures that dwelled within, they would find the shifter soon or later. The shifter did not know if they sought to destroy it or tame it, but it considered neither an option.

As day turned to night, the Kingdom that was ordinarily shrouded in shadow transformed into a Kingdom of impenetrable darkness; moonlight being the only form of illumination for twenty or so miles. Fortunately for the shifter, it needed no light to guide its way as it crept out of the cave mouth, deeming it now safe to do so, and began the steep ascent through the pass under the cover of night. Unfortunately for the beast, the warriors of Shadows Peak did not need light to guide their way either, the shadows whispering to them of the goings-on in the world.

The wind howled through the pass as the wolf began the long trek towards the nearest town. Its stomach grumbled from hiding amongst the wolf pack for several days without food. It was hunger that made the wolf risk the trek this night. Icicles hung from its cloak of white fur, blending in with the freshly fallen snow, the wolf's night vision guiding its way.

The faint smell of smoke was carried on the wind, likely from a burning hearth in one of the watch towers hidden amongst the jagged mountain peaks. The temptation to seek out one of the towers and steal its next meal grew more and more appealing as it continued trekking through the night, padding through the deep snow, mile by never-ending mile. But the shifter was not yet desperate enough to attempt stealing from those warriors who wished nothing more than to rid the mountains of the beast. The shifter would likely gain a stab wound or worse for its troubles, and despite the shifter's unusually quick healing capabilities, it did not want to risk it.

The miles dragged on, the cold sapping its energy despite the thick coat the shifter bore. It found itself growing sloppy in its movements. Its breathing grew labored from the grueling travel and lack of sustenance, its temper rising in turn. It was times like these that the shifter considered growing wings and flying instead. However, the strong winds and billowing snow would make the flight too dangerous, especially at night. A bird could fly straight into a mountain peak if their vision were too obstructed by the relentless snow, or they would risk ice building upon their wings, weighing them down, making it difficult to fly at all. No, a bird was not an option in the current circumstances.

Scaling down a mountain, the shifter felt the ground and snow begin to tremble beneath its feet. The shifter had experienced the sensation only once before and knew trouble was coming. Abandoning all caution, the shifter began sprinting down the mountainside, trying to outrun the wave of snow it knew would be coming.

The ground grumbled now, shaking beneath the wolf's paws as it ran for its life. The wolf risked a glance back up the mountainside, and right at the top he faintly saw them. A group of warriors using their magic to trigger the oncoming avalanche.

Faster, faster the shifter sped, knowing it would not be long until the snow gave way and began its furious descent.

The snow at the mountain peak broke away, and a roar like a gushing wind echoed in the shifter's ears as the snow began pummeling down the mountainside, the shifter in its path. Moments later the shifter lost its footing and the wave of snow crashed against its body, a weight that shattered bones upon impact. Under the wave of snow, it was washed away, darkness enveloping it as the shifter's luck ran out and only death answered its call for help.

*

The shifter awoke on a dais of bones, black billowing smoke floating around it, trailing from the gown of a woman he did not know. A crown of bone perched upon her midnight-colored hair, which was akin to serpents writhing. Sharp claws descended from her fingers. The female's emerald gaze pierced into the shifter's very core, a wicked grin revealing brutal jagged teeth.

The shifter scrambled onto its paws, surprised to find it felt no pain. It was then that the shifter noticed it was floating above the surface, its limbs transparent as if it were... Dead.

A ghost. No, not a ghost... A bhoot.

"Welcome, my pet bhoot," the Lady of Malice proclaimed. "I am Nushka, the Goddess of Blood and Bone. I am your master. Here in The Pitts. you will be more than you ever dreamed of. By my side, you will be free to reach your full, gloriously wicked potential. You will imitate creatures of nightmares. You will be feared, and you will be *mine*. Welcome to The Pitts of Moor. Welcome to eternity."

With a click of the Goddess's fingers, the shifter-turned-bhoot returned to its corporal form, though it still floated on an invisible cloud above the surface. The bhoot roared in glorious wonder at the destiny they had landed upon from their unfortunate demise. The Goddess smiled wickedly in return, as if they were the answer to some unholy prayer for her as well.

THE RISE
OF
HYACINTH

A prequel short story of
The Immortal Deities

Nattie Kate Mason

Concealed deep within the forest of an insignificant mortal kingdom, the wendigast race danced and drank amongst the bonfires. Wine overflowing, the immortal race feasted upon the mortals sacrificed to them, in exchange for the nearby town's safety during the dark gathering.

The wendigast preferred the taste of human hearts, the delicacy rejuvenating their strength and power. However, during the festivities they gorged on whatever they could find. Each clan leader dined on human hearts with their jagged teeth, tearing through flesh and muscle. Their subordinates fed on the leftovers.

Beltane marked the annual gathering of the half-witch, half-spirit race. With long gangly limbs, branch-like arms, cobweb-thin hair, and gaunt features, the immortals were the first of witch-kind to exist in the mortal realm. The magically gifted race was created from the darkest imaginings of The Goddess of Bone and Bone, who reigned over The Pitts of Moor, a place of refuge for the depraved immortals. It was a place of unending pain for wretched mortal souls, deemed unworthy of eternity in the Afterworld.

Hyacinth, the centuries-old daughter of the wendigast leader, Queen Thanatosia, sat perched upon a boulder with preternatural stillness. Blood stained her pursed lips, the lingering taste of fresh blood and a young mortal's heart electrifying her senses and invigorating her powers. Hyacinth's vibrant green eyes overlooked her soon-to-be subjects with a mix of contempt and smug satisfaction.

Her tall stature—even for the abnormally tall race—made her an imposing sight. A gown of plated bark adorned her body; the preferred uniform of her species and a symbol of their close attachment and dependency upon nature. Beneath her gown, a selection of her weapons—mostly daggers and vials of poisons—were strapped to her gangly legs. One vial had already found its new home inside the stomach of one of her intended challengers this evening. The recipient, an obnoxious young wendigast whose aspirations far reached beyond her capabilities, likely lay in the bushes somewhere out of sight, frothing at the mouth, an immortal no longer.

Tonight's celebration marked a change of power, the position of High Witch shifting from one leader to another. After Thanatosia met her premature demise the previous week, under circumstances that could only be considered highly suspicious, Hyacinth would be crowned the new leader. There were no other daughters to contest her, and any suspicions over Thanatosia's death were not spoken of.

Hyacinth had not grieved her late mother's passing, nor did anyone expect her to. Any sign of weakness was intolerable amongst the long-living race and would be considered especially dangerous for a new leader trying to establish her seat of power.

Nearby, two ancient crones were tasked with keeping the bonfires controlled with their giftings. Fire to warm and inspire, but not to burn. If left unchecked, the fire would be devastating for the part-tree spirit race. But the element of danger also enhanced the excitement of the event, especially amongst the younger wendigast.

The energy was electric amongst witchlings; those witnessing their first Beltane gathering with their clan. Many were eager to see how the events of the night would unfold, as it was likely the first and last ascension many wendigast would witness in their lifetimes. Many wendigast lives were not as long-lasting as that of the Royal bloodline.

The power had shifted from Thanatosia to Hyacinth, of that everyone was sure. However, tradition demanded that any who wished to challenge the new ruler's seat of power may do so at her ascension. As new leaders were appointed so rarely, Hyacinth was sure that more than a few were eager to challenge her this night, and for that reason, she kept her wits about her. Not a drop of wine had reached her lips. Her potential opponents could not say the same. Of all gathered, only the witchlings, Hyacinth's personal guards, and her Lady's Maids were free of liquor's influence.

A horn sounded, and the wendigast halted their dancing and revelry. The time had come for the new Queen to ascend.

Hyacinth rose gracefully from her perch atop the boulder, eight of her personal guards appearing by her side as if summoned on a phantom breeze. A show of such force was not needed for the leader's protection, for she was more than capable of protecting herself. Their presence, however, was a demonstration of strength, promising a quick death to anyone threatening to challenge Hyacinth's reign.

As Hyacinth approached the center of the gathering, her bark-plated skirts rustled against the first green grass of spring, her wisplike hair trailing behind her. She climbed upon a stage erected between the two main bonfires, her guards falling into line around her, creating a barrier at the base of the tower. The witchlings whispered amongst themselves as their excitement grew. Snickers from Hyacinth's enemies failed to unruffle the future High Witch, who was never without a trick up her sleeve.

The clan's Priestess, Cyrene, the correspondent between the Goddess of Blood and Bone and the wendigast, hunched over her engraved, red wood cane, her eyes the color of a raging storm. Upon the Priestess's gown of plated bark, a thousand years of built-up moss had grown. Insects and spiders had made their homes amongst her skirts. Her cobweb-like hair was so matted, not a single strand was distinguishable amongst the rest. But Cyrene paid no heed to her appearance, her focus solely upon fulfilling the role entrusted to her by the Dark Goddess herself.

Hyacinth did not bow before the Priestess, as no Queen would ever bow before a subordinate, though she gave a respectful nod in reverence for the role she would play in tonight's ceremony.

"Tonight, we are gathered as the Goddess has demanded to appoint our new leader," Priestess Cyrene declared. "The Dark Goddess of Blood and Bone approves of Hyacinth's rise, but as tradition demands, let any who oppose this ascension step forward and claim your right to challenge her reign in the form of a battle to the death."

Suspense and excitement built as more than ten wendigast approached the base of the stage and unsheathed their weapons, declaring their intentions.

A crone dressed in fighting leathers, who went by the name of Shakara, boldly approached the stage stairs, close enough to share breath with Hyacinth's head guard.

"I challenge you, Hyacinth!" Shakara declared, for despite her age, she was strong, powerful, and still stood a chance of defeating the wendigast heir.

Hyacinth's grin grew. Her jagged teeth gleamed as she approached the edge of the stage and stared down her opponent.

"I would expect nothing less from you... *Shakara*. But heed my warning, I have no intention of losing my seat of power today or *ever*," the future leader proclaimed.

Hyacinth tilted her head to the side, sizing up her prey, but she made no attempt to reach for her weapons. Instead, she stared knowingly towards her age-old opponent and chanted an ancient phrase under her breath.

Shakara dropped her weapons immediately, her skin paling. She reached for her neck, suddenly unable to breathe, but it was over before it began. She began frothing at the mouth just as her body dropped to the floor, shuddering as her powers drained from her body, her lifeforce leaking out and returning to the ground. Her soul transported to the realm of the Goddess of Darkness, where she would officially await her eternal judgment, before being entrusted into the Goddess of Blood and Bone's care in The Pits of Moor for all eternity.

The Pitts of Moor is the opposite of The Land of Milk and Honey for depraved souls such as the wendigast. An eternal resting place for departed souls with sinful natures, craving depravity. The Dark Goddess's realm is a place where wicked souls are free to realize their full, sinful potential without reproach.

Smirks turned into angered hisses as the other challengers took in their fellow competitor's fate.

"How dare you!" One of the challengers seethed as she stepped over Shakara's lifeless body, trying to push past Hyacinth's guard and take on the future ruler in combat.

Before the next challenger could take one more step towards the top of the stage, Hyacinth mumbled her incantation again and the next bold witch slumped dead upon the stairs.

Hyacinth raised her head proudly and stared down her nose at the remaining competitors.

"I will not be defeated. Heed my warning. Lay down your arms or you will meet the same fate as our dark sisters," Hyacinth brazenly declared.

Hyacinth could have given her challengers more than a moment to reconsider their opposition and drop their weapons before delivering their punishment. But as she knew all too well, fear invoked power.

"FACTOREM OCCURSUM TUUM!" Hyacinth bellowed.

At the foot of the stage, not only the remaining challengers, but all who had been known to oppose Hyacinth's reign, met their swift demise. Crumpling to the floor in a wave of death, hundreds of wendigast met their premature ends. If the fools had been more wary, they would have noticed the slight tang of the magical tonic lacing their wine, awaiting activation by the wendigast leader's chant, designed to affirm her place as Ruler for as long as she may live.

To eliminate such a large proportion of your own people may seem unfathomable to mortal folk, a crime punishable by death. But for the depraved worshippers of the Goddess of Blood and Bone, it was merely a matter of ensuring one's survival.

The remaining wendigast fell to their knees in submission to their new leader, and thus a dark legend was born: Hyacinth, Queen and High Witch of all tree-spirit and witch kind.

Acknowledgements

It takes a tribe to publish a book and I couldn't be more grateful for the team that supports me. Thank you to Chloe and Aidan, for turning my ramblings into a piece of art that I can be proud of. Thank you for always pushing me to grow my craft. I learn so much with each book I write, and this book was no exception.

Thank you to Beth for once again bringing my dreams to life in this cover. Your talent is phenomenal. I am so thankful to have you creating my amazing covers.

Thank you to Helen, for helping write such an amazing blurb. Your wealth of experience, friendship and wise advice is always appreciated.

Thank you to Jess for doing the final proofread. Your fresh eyes were invaluable at picking up those final little errors.

Thank you to my husband. Through the sleepless and stressful nights, you have always been there to encourage me and bring me cups of tea. I am so grateful for all your support.

To my friends and family, thank you for always encouraging me, and pushing me through the hard times. Without your support, this book would not be finished.

Thank you to Lily. Though you are too young to read this book, thank you for allowing mummy the time to work on her book. Thank you for your patience and for all the times your have missed out on 'fun mummy,' so that I could keep working. I love you more than you will ever know.

Finally, thank you to my readers. Without you, I couldn't keep doing the job I love. I am so grateful for all your positive reviews and shout-outs on Instagram. I am thankful to every one of you that loves my characters and helps spread the word about my books. I am so grateful to each one of you for your endless support.

Lastly, thank you to my close friends and fellow authors, who encourage me no matter what. Thank you to Ruthy and Kayla, for always having my back and for always being my number one cheerleaders. My life is so much fuller for having you ladies in it.

Thank you everyone,

Nattie x

About the Author

Nattie Kate Mason is an Australian self-published author. Nattie works as a nurse in her day job, but her passions are reading and writing. Nattie has travelled around Australia with her little family of three, living in various towns and cities.

Life is never dull for Nattie and her unique little family. Nature, life and reading, help to inspire Nattie's creative side. You will often find her outside reading a good book, whilst enjoying a cup of tea.

The Goddess of Blood and Bone, is Nattie's debut New Adult Fantasy novel. Nattie is looking forward to bringing the sequel to her readers in 2022.

To see where Agnes's story began, check out The Crowning YA Fantasy series.

Other titles by Nattie Kate Mason:

The Crowning young adult fantasy series:

The Crowning

A Queen's Fate

Heart of a Crown

Visit nattiekatemason.com to stay up to date on the latest new releases from this author.